Dead Man Talking
Famous Last Words of F.C. Naylor

by

Luke Sorba

DORRANCE PUBLISHING CO., INC.
PITTSBURGH, PENNSYLVANIA 15222

ISBN: 978-1-4349-0937-4
eISBN: 978-1-4349-5779-5
Printed in the United States of America

First Printing

For more information or to order additional books, please contact:
Dorrance Publishing Co., Inc.
701 Smithfield Street
Pittsburgh, Pennsylvania 15222
U.S.A.
1-800-788-7654
www.dorrancebookstore.com

Dedication

For Renato and Milena.

Do not go gentle into that good night.
Rage, rage against the dying of the light.
—Dylan Thomas (1952)

Foreword

FC Naylor - playwright, commentator, class warrior, and Pub Quiz runner-up, was first introduced to me in person by a fellow literary agent in the bar of the Tricycle Theatre, in Kilburn, London during a packed and well-lubricated Irish Poets Evening. My first impressions were of a belligerent, highly intelligent demagogue full of anger and hurt, but also of immense acuity and bitter proto-Homeric wisdom. When my eyes first fell on Naylor, he was physically wrestling with a spike-haired barman in a heated dispute over whether the peanuts in a dish on the bar were for all patrons or just those who had paid for their drinks. As verbal bombshells and occasional physical ones sallied between this erstwhile man of letters in his threadbare corduroy jacket and the pimpled part-timer in his North London Poly sweatshirt, I was reminded of the inexhaustible passion that characterized Naylor's crash-and-burn years as a polemical playwright in the late seventies and early eighties. The disabling *cri de Coeur,* which erupted Banshee-like from all his former works, could be heard in everything Naylor did. And, as the two public bar pugilists tumbled down onto the beer-stained carpet in a cloud of cigarette ash and alcohol spray, trading punches and profanities like a flea market Foreman and Ali, it was that quality of sincerity, as raw and rare as a Sumatran tiger in this age of literary peacocks and chameleons, that made up my mind. "I am going to sign that man up, if he dries out," I said to my companion.

"Oh, he's not drunk," she replied. "He's always like that."

Because publishers were harassing me more than mendicants from a Cairo souk, forcing me to don a series of ever more improbable disguises for my lunchtime sojourns to the Groucho Club (five of my clients—a footballer, two soap stars, a runner-up in *The Intern* and the winner of *Celebrity Rehab Archipelago* — were all severely behind deadlines with their autobiographies, which means they can't even get it together to mail their old school photos to their ghostwriters) I ultimately decided not to take a chance on this loon. However, on the grounds that: 1) it was I who, pro bono, drew up the contract for his newspaper column, and 2) more or less everybody else in his address book were measuring up the prospect of libel suits, it befalls me to write this introduction.

FC Naylor was best known, or more truthfully *only* known, for his 1979 *succes de scandale, Treading on the Peasant Grave* with its infamous depiction of huntsmen pursuing a pheasant-beater and forcing him to eat, page by page, a copy of the *King James Bible*. Written as a riposte to the incarceration of IRA hunger strikers in the Maze prison, it triggered a notorious fistfight between Bernard Levin and David Hare in the stalls of the Royal Court. However, subsequent efforts such as his provocative meditation on the Royal Wedding of Charles and Diana, *Whore;* and the more personal piece, *Gulag 69*, an indictment of the British education system in general and predatory homosexual chemistry teacher, Mr Eagles, in particular (he regularly beat Naylor on the backside with a plimsoll), were both critical and commercial failures.

These disappointments culminated in Naylor's absurdist experimentation called *Weepadeepawoodpeckerway*, which premiered in the open air in Jubilee Gardens1} at the 1986 "Save the GLC" rally. Notwithstanding a lively score for steel pan orchestra by Kevin Rowlands, it prompted the entire audience to demand their money back, despite the event actually being free. Funding for Naylor's final play, the miners' strike drama *Lamplight*—considered by the author as his defining masterpiece—was offered up by the Mirror Group as a tax loss, but eventually sank along with owner, Robert Maxwell, and remains unproduced.

Naylor's career nadir coincided with the breakdown of his marriage and divorce from Camberwell School of Art graduate and bohemian heiress, Lady Cressida Parnell—Lady Parnell acquiring custody of their only son, Danton Vladimir Che Parnell-Naylor.

Thus, a unique voice was silenced and Naylor spent the ensuing years in obscurity serving as a tutor in creative writing at Morley Adult Education College spearheading, in his own words, "the search for the country's next Jeffrey Archer or Andy McNab." Moreover, it was only last year's announcement that Mr. Naylor had been diagnosed with the untreatable degenerative neurological condition *Voltaire's Hippocampic Dysfunction* that caused him to resurface as a blip on the radar of public life.

However, that sad, ill-deserved turn of Fortuna's wheel had unexpected consequences for this hitherto forgotten writer, thinker, and activist and the following collection of incisive, candid, rambling, scurrilous, humorous, and profound diary entries culled from his weekly column in *The Commentator*, which make Samuel Pepys look like Bridget Jones, are the best bounty of the worst luck. Naylor's life may have been close to its end, but suddenly he was back in our lives—fresh, fearless, and contemporary. So hold tight and read the last words of a dying man, every bit as enraged now as he was in that fighting cage of a Circle bar all those years ago, as he refuses go gently into the night.

Sir Claude Seraph-Jones, R.A., O.B.E.

Introduction

I have never written a book before in my life and I'm not going to start now. Chances are, if I had started to write one I would not have lived to see it finished, let alone published. (It's a miracle I am alive enough to write this introduction—well in advance of publication, just in case....) Also, literature has been extinct for decades. There hasn't been a great novel written since Gabriel Garcia Marquez knocked off *100 Years of Solitude* in 1967 and that was in Spanish. The last outstanding English language book was probably *Midnight's Children* by Salman Rushdie. I say *probably* because I haven't read it. I'm all up for burning Rushdie's books too, because they are so long and boring...lecherous, po-faced snob.

Stage plays are what I do, but there's no point to them anymore; anything too long for *YouTube* or too erudite for a junkie on "Meth" will be completely forgotten in fifty years time. The theatre is where the middle classes go to die peacefully. It's the only place in the world now where you can't use a mobile phone, but already texts have started to hum away discreetly. I remember when a man in a theatre draped a raincoat over his lap to hide his erect cock. Now, it's his Blackberry.

No, I'm giving permission in advance for a complete collection of my newspaper articles to be published (which span more or less nine months, referred to by myself as "Naylor's Gestation Period"): 1) to make money for doing nothing even if I won't get a chance to spend it, 2) because I can't do anything about it, the bloody newspaper owns the copyright, and 3) the money again.

Oh, and don't expect me to thank anyone in this introduction. No one involved in this book is in it for anyone but themselves. Therefore, if below you read an acknowledgement of the contribution of my newspaper publisher Cressida Parnell (aka my ex-wife), and newspaper editor Alistair (aka her new husband, aka A Wanker), DISREGARD IT; I guarantee it was in none of the galleys I approved and has been entered COMPLETELY AGAINST MY WILL.

I would like to sincerely acknowledge the contributions made by newspaper publisher Cressida Parnell and editor Alistair Sinclair, without whose unyielding support these weekly columns in *The Commentator* newspaper would never have been written.

FC Naylor

1. Saturday, March 3 (Debut Column)

So I've got to turn in one of these columns every week and make sure they are always *new and exciting*, eh? So it says in the latest email from this esteemed newspaper's visionary editor, Alistair Sinclair, the man who pioneered the insertion (inside the ten-part, ten-kilo Saturday edition) of "The Supplement Supplement: a new and exciting info-and-picture-packed guide to…exciting info-and-picture-packed guides!" But he somehow still managed to find—in the same heroic against-all-odds manner in which Stanley managed to locate Livingstone, Dorothy found Oz, darts champion Andy "The Viking" Fordham found his toes, and Jacqui Smith her soul—space for this *new and exciting half-page column*! Although some of you may have noticed that the weekly "Soft Fruit Puddings of the Massif Central" feature has consequently been reduced to a mere Baker's dozen of recipes, the announcement of which precipitated such a ferocious letter-writing, rail-chaining campaign by the cuckolded wives of Aga-shire (for whom food replaced sex the second the Boeing 737 touched down at Terminal 2 at the end of their honeymoon in Dubai or the Maldives), you would have thought gypsies had moved into their gardens.

Alistair Sinclair, by the way, owes his job entirely to his wife, Lady Cressida Parnell, who happens to own this newspaper (and a substantial part of Aga-shire). But then so do I. I was once married to her too, years before Alistair, when marriage was still *new and exciting*. She was my inspirational muse and I was her hot-headed lover, as opposed to the better-than–nothing-salve-to-loneliness-in-her-later-years spot that Alistair now occupies. Anyway, Cressida told her hubby to give the silenced voice, which she believes that I have become, a weekly column out of pity and so he invited me over.

"What on earth do you want me to write about?" I asked the prudent patrician of Peebles (I had to be direct as the chap was more than a tad distracted by the plastic scale model of the spanking new Richard Rogers'-designed, state-of-the-art premises the newspaper will be moving to next year. Alistair is obsessed with finding the precise piece of Lego that directly corresponds to his own office with its promised overview of Chiswick Mall and St Nicholas's Church with its fifteenth century tower.)

Most of the other columns in this paper are by former staffers on maternity leave, writing about the *new and exciting* discovery that: 1) dragging a bellyful of baby around in an unsympathetic world designed by and for young single men is a bit of fag really... but worth it; that 2) breastfeeding, sleepless nights, and getting your figure back in an unsympathetic world designed by and for young single men is also a bit of fag really... but worth it; and finally 3) that combining work while also raising a child in an unsympathetic world designed by and for young single men is also a bit of fag etc., etc. Except that *writing a column* isn't really work, is it? After which, maternity leave completed, they get their old jobs back and the column is transferred to the next young woman in the Features Department (since childminders don't get columns) to have gotten herself pregnant by one of those aforementioned irksome, young, single men. (Every other column in the paper is some bloke complaining about what he saw on television.)

I could also write about parenthood, I suppose. I am the father of one son, now aged twenty-three, Danton Vladimir Che Naylor-Parnell (although he now insists on calling himself "Toby" and earning his living as a Yacht salesman for New Atlantic Marina Ltd. in Newport, California, which ironically is on the Pacific Coast. But then Americans are notorious for their ignorance of geography, which is why so many of their troops keep absentmindedly wandering across the border into places like Korea, Vietnam, Nicaragua, Iraq, Afghanistan, and "Holy shit, I could have sworn this was Rhode Island" Guam.) Perhaps my column could lift the lid on combining fatherhood, working in the arts, and managing an indulged aristocratic ex-wife poisoned by a lethal cocktail of high anxiety and low self-esteem. Or, I could come up with something that won't kill me with boredom while writing it, even more quickly than it kills you with boredom when reading it.

By the way, you should know that is how I got this column—the death bit; I am dying.

Learning about my impending death motivated that pity that drove Cressida belatedly to grant me this column, which is bad news for me, given that I like living. And, worse news for you because: 1) A dying man stops caring about the consequences of what he says, and 2) no citizen, and I mean none, of our beloved country with its unique history of reverence for the very poorly (and domestic pets), would dare try to stop a dying man from writing exactly what he wants.

Ha, ha, and ha.

FC Naylor

2. Saturday, March 10

I'm back and it has been quite a week. I have had a bit of a to-do with my upstairs neighbor, Pavla, that has made life a bit more difficult and there have been repercussions since my debut column was published that has made work, well, both better and worse, really. On the one hand, none of the female staff at the paper are talking to me after my innocent remarks about maternity leave…that's the good news. The bad news is that Alistair insists I write something about my illness.

I said, "Surely you don't think that your readership, educated and compassionate as they are, want to read a blow-by-blow graphic account of my physical and mental degeneration as I am dragged slowly and helplessly toward death like a house-mouse in a cat's maw? Surely your readers are not the sort of people who read Patricia Cornwell and Martina Cole in order to gorge their over-privileged palates on forensic descriptions of the minutiae of bodily suffering like modern day rakes and dolls on a day trip to Bedlam."

But he said that you are and you would. So, just this once, here it is.

After some problems with balance—not BBC-style balance, i.e., for every NASA astrophysicist on the show discussing oscillations in the sun's magnetic field there must be a member of the Flat Earth Society warning the citizens of Spitsbergen to stay indoors or risk stepping off the edge of the world. Or, if you have

Noam Chomsky on the show discussing racism and U.S. foreign policy, you need to have the Imperial Wizard of the Tennessee Ku Klux Klan putting a dissenting view and going on about "uppity niggers."

Not that type of balance. I'm talking wobbly legs and spilling my venti-decaff-no-cream-mocha over a baby in *Starbucks,* which set me back three quid and a *reluctant* apology (babies shouldn't be allowed near coffee, decaf or otherwise, if you ask me). After that I decided I needed checking over, so I had my best friend Adam Gold do it. Fortunately, Adam also happens to be a doctor rather than an actuary or golf pro, so I actually ended up with a useful diagnosis instead of a cure for the yips or a new tax code. Unfortunately, we know all of each other's secrets (he blames his mother for stopping him from pursuing a career in musical theatre and deliberately keeps meat and dairy on the *same* shelf in the fridge to annoy her), so it's very hard to disguise bad news.

"FC, I'm afraid the blood test has come up positive for Voltaire's Hippocampic Disorder," he told me, rather smugly, I thought.

"Oh, is that what Voltaire died of?" I asked. I like the idea of having something in common with a fellow *homme des belles lettres,* even if only the way he snuffed it.

"You know I can't comment on another doctor's patient," he answered. Now you should know that Adam qualifies as my best friend only in as much as he is my *only* friend. I'm afraid I've lost almost as many friends as I have bets and hair. Actually, according to *Wikipedia,* Voltaire died from a very painful and chronic urinary infection, so perhaps I am better off this way. Turns out the condition of VHD has nothing to do with the scion of the *Enlightenment,* but was named after a doctor named Voltaire who discovered it. Talk about exploiting other people's misery to get your place in history. The likes of Alois Alzheimer, Burrill Crohn, Hans Creutzfeldt, Alfons Jakob, and whatever Mr. Non-Hodgkins' first name is, would *never* have become household names if it weren't for people like me. Sick people. Gravely sick. Pronounce a death sentence—or at least one of chronic ill health—and you get famous off it. These are vultures, not scientists. Medical pioneers who identify a new and terrible disease just to get themselves into the dictionary and then bugger off without thinking about, maybe—I don't know—*curing* it. Sod 'em, I say! And as for you, George Albert Edouard Brutus Gilles de la Tourette—*I* would swear out loud uncontrollably if my middle name were Brutus, too.

So, that is all you are getting. If you thought this was going to be one of those diaries about stool inspections or MRI scans, forget it, get your ghoulish fun on cable from *Grey's Anatomy* or *When Extreme Genital Piercings Go Wrong*. All you need to know about my illness is what Adam told me when I asked how long I had to live.

"If you look after yourself—eat well, exercise, and lay off the booze—two years," he answered.

"So, how long have *I* got?"

"Nine months."

"Really?"

"No. More like six."

Yes, dear reader, make the most of this column now because in less than nine months time it will be no more, because in less than nine months time, I will be no more either.

Armed with that knowledge, the day after my diagnosis I went straight to *Comet* on the Old Kent Road and bought £12,000 worth of home entertainment system, computers, and a dishwasher—all on a "buy now, pay nothing for a year" plan.

Finally, if you are wondering how my scandalous portrayal of both my boss and my benefactor last week managed to get printed uncensored, it was because Alistair Sinclair foolishly expected it would sufficiently provoke Mrs. Boss (Cressida) into withdrawing her patronage. However, the Scottish sage was wrong. Instead, Lady Parnell proclaimed that the opinions of yours truly, however misguided, were honestly felt and, therefore, merited airing in a newspaper that has prided itself for ten generations on its pluralism of views. Personally, I think it was really because she got a tingle in a private place recalling all that never-to-be-equalled, booze-fuelled, make-up sex the two of us had in the seventies and early eighties. Although, Alistair, I understand you feel quite safe that all your selfless *New Man* helping-out in the kitchen with the clootie dumplings, shavings of Japanese gingko root, and drizzles of cold-pressed virgin olive oil, more than makes up for the absence of raw, unadulterated lust.

Don't you?

FC Naylor

3. Saturday, March 17 (Extended Column)

An interesting few days…

<u>Monday</u>

Vanessa, my editor's secretary, rings to give me the good news that I have more space for my column than previous weeks. The Union of Myanmar is withdrawing the eight-page "Why Naypyidaw Is the Ideal Location for a Holiday, Business Conference, Trade Agreement, or Business Investment," because their *Head of the Foreign Relations and International Commerce Liaison Department* is indisposed. For "indisposed," read, "suddenly executed for crimes against the state," or so it says on the Reuters' website, which is ironic because his "crime against the state" was—logging onto the Reuters' website.

After I tell Vanessa (by the way I've no idea if Alistair's secretary is actually called Vanessa; I can never remember her name and "Vanessa" seemed as likely as any other name. Besides, she is a kind soul and likely to put my forgetting her name down to my brain condition as opposed to my perennial self-absorption) that: 1) I will not bail out Alistair and fill up eight blank pages because he's been let down at the last minute by the Burmese military junta or the "State Peace and Development Council," as they style themselves in the century's most paradoxical euphemism since the Americans named "killing your own men and their allies because you are too stupid, too cowardly, too reckless, too gung ho, or all of the above to check first," *friendly* fire; and 2) I haven't done eight pages of stuff in eight years, let alone a week!

At this point, Alistair gets on the line and shouts that if I am going to write a column I have to start *doing things* to write about. So, since Adam is on a home visit, I ask Pavla in the flat above for advice. Pavla is a kind, modest, and pretty twenty-five-year-old Pole from Gdansk (home of 1980s political titan and shipbuilder, Lech Walesa about whom Pavla knows bugger all) who, contrary to my conclusion-jumping ex-wife who once stumbled across Pavla alone with me in my flat upon a rare visit, is *not* a prostitute. As I explained to her Ladyship, Ms. Borowcyck (a name she shares with transgressive 1970s film director and iconoclast, Walerian Borowcyck about whom Pavla knows bugger all) was a finalist in the Polish National Spelling Bee, speaks three languages, and has a degree in metallurgical engineering and, therefore, has no need to turn to prostitution. She is a nanny.

If I had a daughter, I would want her to be like Pavla. And, if I had a lover, I would also want her to be like Pavla…though clearly not at the same time. (Sometimes Cressida's snobbery riles me so much I want her to give back her key to my flat, but as I pay my rent to her (she bought it off the Council using the Right-to-Buy legislation that I abhor and charges me peppercorn rent), that's not an option—besides, she probably has copies.

Anyway, Pavla has been visiting me regularly ever since she heard that I was dying, mainly to check up on me, but partly, I suspect, to get away from her overcrowded apartment, which she shares with a Russian, a Czech, and a Ukrainian in order to save money, even though all they have in common is broken English and a reflex hatred of Germans and Napoleon. Pavla is always encouraging me to do more in order to enrich my final months, while simultaneously taking my mind off the fact that these are my final months.

Unfortunately, going out with Pavla nearly always entails going out with Millimant and Mirabell, too. Yes, I too initially thought they must be poodles. They are, in fact, the twin son and daughter of Pavla's employers, for whom Pavla is paid to provide daytime care while Daddy is busy managing a hedge fund in the city and mummy is busy being a magistrate, taking fencing lessons, and having sex with an actor. Adam, whose fondness for theatre first drew us together at Lancaster University where I was a post-grad and he an undergraduate, tells me the children are actually named after characters in a Restoration play. I told him, playwright I may be, but I refuse to read the work of anyone whose patrons brought to an end Britain's only ever experiment at being a republic.

Adam is also irked that I won't watch all those TV talent shows that he and his wife love to watch together. I told him as soon as Andrew Lloyd Webber agrees to front, "How Do You Solve a Problem Like *The Good Woman of Szechuan?*" I'll volunteer to be on the panel.

Thankfully, Pavla is in—with the kids, too. I had suspected such earlier when my room suddenly went dark as if there had been an unannounced eclipse of the sun. In fact, her employers' 4-wheel drive was parked outside and completely blocked all light coming through my window…and I live on the first floor. You could solve London's overcrowding by sheltering all of the city's homeless under a single wheel arch. The ridiculous car is called a Volkswagen Touareg. The Touaregs…those desert-dwelling, subsistence farmers of North Africa, famous for swordsmanship, camels, and, of course, their top-of-the-line sports utility vehicles with 5-litre engines, power steering, twin air bags, and anthracite leather trim. (*All* car manufacturers are arses.)

Tuesday

In order to meet Alistair's demands sent via "Vanessa" (it's too late to admit to her now that I don't know what she is really called, so I'm going to have to stick with this one), I have agreed to accompany Pavla to the City Farm for a day out with M and M in order to generate material. (I never got the chance to take Danton/Toby to a City Farm when he was little, mainly because of living in the country where there are so many real farms).

Interesting place, the Farm, as it turns out—full of farm animals, mostly friendly. Staff, too. Shame I can't say the same thing about the other parents. First, one mum complained about the sandwich I was eating; claimed my turkey slices would upset the poultry. So, I told her I was perfectly happy throwing it away…as soon as she took off her leather boots, belt, gloves, coat, and handbag, which were distressing to the cows, as well as being obviously intended for a much younger woman. She muttered something in Italian, which I initially took to be some exotic cuss word she picked up skiing in the Dolomites, but Pavla informed me it was the name of a fashion designer. Fortunately, our dialogue was interrupted by an attractive, *resting* actress kitted out in dung brown overalls—chosen to blend in with the pavement, I imagine—who enthusiastically introduced everyone to "Wally, the two-year-old Harris hawk."

Annoyingly, the same mother piped up again when the guide asked if any of the children could name another bird of prey. "Eagle", she cried. What a big word for a graduate in her late thirties, I thought. (Pavla insists I said it out loud, but I couldn't be sure).

"One of the children, please." The guide reiterates politely. Then without blinking, another mum whispers the answer into little Joshua's, or Seth's, or Nebuchadnezzar's (or some such Old Testament name) ear. So, of course, I called her on it and she denied it. Straight out lied. Then the guide, who by now must have wished she had taken up that waitressing or temping offer between roles instead, calls out, "Any other birds of prey, children? Maybe one beginning with *V*?" and the same stupid woman whispers, "Crow!" Crow! Not only does it not begin with *V*, it's not even a bird of prey! It's a large passerine.

"You can't even cheat properly, woman," I observed. That's when they all turned on me. Pavla begged them to forgive me because I was dying, but I soon wiped those grudging frowns of sympathy off their shiny Botoxed foreheads when I pulled little Aaron, or Caleb, or Habakkuk out of his buggy. But, as I explained to the police officer later, the day was meant to be a chance for deprived city children to look at some animals but, no, this coven of shrieking hide-clad progenitrices has to turn it into the bloody Oxbridge Entrance Exam. And, not only were the parents cheating, they were giving the kids the wrong information.

Not that that matters to these people. Because if all those carrot, pomegranate, and goji smoothies and Omega-3 oils they force-feed their kids so they can memorize Pi to one hundred significant figures and see in the dark at the same time, don't get them into the best schools—the private Latin tutor, the cello lessons, and paying for a new stained-glass window at the local church should. And they *have* to go to the best schools, don't they? Because only then can they go to the *best* universities and get the *best*-paid jobs, which none of them need, of course! In fact, should they not rather step aside and make way for the poor children, who actually need jobs to *earn a living*. These rich kids are just waiting 'til 2029 when they'll be able to sell their parents' four-story Georgian terrace in NW1 for ten zillion million pounds and buy their own Channel Island! Or, get together with some equally rich friends and terraform their own planet!

That's why I decided to liberate the little darlings and scooped up a few of them, jumped over a turnstile, and we all galloped across a field together like in Rousseau's *Emile* but, of course, all the mums had sodding off-road vehicles and before I knew it, I was surrounded by jeering termagants who demanded I be arrested as a pedophile. Of course, not one of them could pick out her own child after I had "muddled them all up" because they were all wearing identical Boden duffle coats and the same soulless thousand-mile stare! Luckily, they dropped the charges when Pavla's employer turned up at the station. Maybe it is handy knowing a beak after all.

FC Naylor

P.S. Finally, I remember Alistair's secretary is called, not Vanessa but…Michael. I know, but he does have a seriously high voice.

4. Saturday, March 24

Got into trouble for last week's column, but not from the expected sources—not from Alistair, though I'm pretty confident I made him seethe inside. Well not sure about *seething*, not sure if seething is in that Edinburgh Presbyterian's emotional range, which makes Kelly Brook's look like Meryl Streep's. He'll be experiencing something less virile, consternation perhaps; the same emotion he might feel should Cressida beat him at Scrabble. Of course back then, "Mustard" and I used to play strip-Scrabble with two items off for a double-word score, three for a triple, and the lot for a seven-letter word and, by the way, Alistair, no that's not where the game finished. That's where it started to get interesting…

No reprisals from Alistair's secretary either, although his voice seems mysteriously to have dropped more octaves than Aled Jones's.

Would you believe it? The grief I got was from Adam! Apparently his mum got hold of the piece through her weekly Bridge ("Bourgeois Bingo," I call it) partner and she asked Adam if it was true what I said about him being railroaded into being a doctor? He responded to her with the murky ambivalence of all GPs ("Lovely day, Doctor". "Hmm, let's wait 'til the tests come back before we jump to conclusions, shall we?") Next thing I know, *la mère* Gold is on the line to *me* crying. Well, regardless of her advanced years and (self-diagnosed) frail health, I had to be honest with her.

"Yes, Esther." (I think she's called Esther, although that might be Adam's wife's name. I get the two mixed up and—between you and me—they do, too.) "Your only son will forever regret you gagging his creative expression and nixing him living life in-the-moment as an actor."

His mum weeps some more. "But, if you hadn't," I add "he would only have ended up alone, penniless and forgotten like me, instead of married with children and a well-paid, high status job-for-life as a doctor. It was the best thing a mother ever could have done him!"

After which, she told me she would light a menorah for me (that's seven times the protection a Catholic mother would have given me with their single candle…yet people whine Jews are stingy!). Plus, the next day what does Kwame from Parcel Force bring me? Two kilos of fish balls cooked in matzo meal, that's what. Bless you Mrs. G and shame on your ungrateful son (who, if he had indeed become an actor, would not have needed to live vicariously through me, and then where would our friendship be?)

Enough of that now. I don't want this column ending up being all about…this column. The media is self-referential enough already, Ouroboros eating it's own tail, only think less giant myth-ical serpent as a metaphor for eternity and more *fluke worm* re-sponsible for exciting TV listings like, "On *Behind the Scenes* this week, we visit the set of the *Making of…* special feature on the newly-released bonus DVD of *So You Want to Be a TV Presenter?* —the TV show in which a member of the public is chosen to present the TV series, *Behind the Scenes!*"

Yeurgh, cough, spit…is that the taste of my own scaly arse in my mouth?

No, this week I encountered for the first time *a little known fact*. I know that's not as newsworthy as encountering *a well-known person*, but here goes. Significantly more chronically ill people die *on the toilet* than in a hospital bed. That's absolutely true. Elvis Presley was not an aberration. Apparently, straining on the loo can often overwhelm a weakened heart and I am not ashamed of admitting that since I found this out I have been in bit of a panic, if not to say completely constipated. Time was I was fully prepared to take on any size of rough-hewn ambulance man *mano a mano* to avoid getting driven to hospital where you have to admit the stats for leaving alive are not on our side. But now I discover my most dangerous enemy is not the paramedic, but my own poo.

As a result, first thing Monday, well ten o'clock (I stayed up for test match highlights the night before), I emptied the house of anything resembling roughage. Luckily, there never having been any whole meal bread, bran cereal, salad vegetables, unprocessed pulses, or fresh fruit in the house to begin with, made that task less arduous than expected and by 10:05 I was staring at a long empty day ahead.

Pavla was at the Early Learning Centre, so I was alone in the building. The shops beckoned and I legged it to Sainsbury's at Dog Kennel Hill, gliding past a street urchin playfully setting off the automatic doors, and went in search of extra starchy foods and, should that fail, enough Imodium to paralyze the bowels of a police horse. However, I hadn't reckoned on what happened the night before.

Prior to my visit to the www.Death_is_an_Inconvenience.com (geddit?) website, I had eaten a rather nourishing and tasty Lamb Rogan Josh from Camberwell's finest curry house (still), the New Dewaniam. (If only England had been touring Australia instead of India, I probably would have eaten some bowel-blocking steak in barbecue sauce.) So, by the time I reach Aisle 9, I knew I had to go to the toilet. Not wishing to die alone, I, of course, rang Adam on my mobile, but he had a waiting room of back complaints and mild depression wanting to be signed-off from work. I then speed-dialled Cressida, only to find her at the acupuncturist receiving treatment for a back complaint and mild depression. I even tried Alistair, but it looks like Michael/Vanessa has taken umbrage after all, and when I told that secretarial Orlando what my problem was, he/she hung up laughing. That left the Virgin Mobile operator, a very sympathetic, educated young lady most eager to help. Unfortunately, she was speaking from a Call Centre in Bangalore and wasn't able to get a flight over in time.

By this stage, I was desperate in both senses of the word, so I threw myself at the mercy of the Community. I only wanted someone to stand outside the cubicle in case something happened, but you would have thought I was asking them to bear me a child. Customer Service said she couldn't leave her post, but offered to double my Nectar points. A tall, strapping shelf-stacker whom I picked out because he looked like he could easily lift me if I fell unconscious on the bog, called me a "Batty Man" and aimed a trolley full of carbonated water at me. Then I remembered back in the days when I used to park my Allegro on the Trinity Close Estate just north of Stamford Bridge, you could pay a kid two and six to keep an eye on your car for the duration of the match. But when I asked the scruffy, little lad I saw earlier (who had by now moved onto harassing elderly customers and clumsily trying to shuck pound coins from shopping trolleys) if he minded waiting outside the toilet for me, he demanded a "tenner." Ten bloody quid! When I threatened to tell his Truant Officer he was not at school, he threatened to tell his Social Worker that I was a pervert. The dreary prospect of being falsely accused of pedophilia twice in the same week did, however, cause my bowel urges to abate. Not my sense of justice, however, and I told the young person, "You may be only eleven—or at a stretch a poorly nourished fourteen—but you are also a disrespectful, thieving extortionist," and kicked him. The boy, after overcoming his surprise at being challenged by anyone, let alone a skinny man in late middle age, was about to launch at me, but it would appear the Olympian shelf-stacker had changed his opinion of me and successfully intervened. I left the store a hero.

I've now tackled my fear of dying on the toilet by training myself to go in the evening when Pavla is back from work and setting up a chair for her outside my toilet door. To discourage her chatting to me, which makes me take longer–like most men, when on the loo (to paraphrase the odious *Top Gun*), I feel the need, the need to read. I have bought Pavla an iPod and Wi-Fi laptop computer (on 12 months' credit, *bien sur!*), so that she can catch up with the latest tunes or keep up with her Facebook friends while I do what I need to do. I like to think there's something in it for both of us.

That's it for this week. Got to go…literally.

FC Naylor

5. Saturday, March 30

It's April Fool's Day tomorrow, so I should really be using this opportunity to announce some fictitious event like "Open Day at MI5 HQ," or invent some bogus story like "Victoria Beckham Finishes Meal" and have a good laugh at your expense, but since most of what you read in the papers between March 31 and April 2 is already made up, why make a fuss about today? Instead, I am entitling today's edition of my column as "The Issue about My Issue with My Issue" (using three alternative definitions of the word issue—clever, eh?)

On Sunday, at noon exactly, my phone went and my 23-year-old U.S.-domiciled, ignoble, cozener of a son Toby rang. Since I have heard less from Toby in these last few years than Beethoven did in his, and I am poorer than Mozart in his, this was not going to be a call of the "Hi, Dad, got any cash?" variety. Briefly, I fantasized it is a life-changing announcement, such as, "Dad, I am flying out to help the newly-elected Maoist Prime Minister of Nepal bring change to his people," or a somewhat less unlikely, "Dad, I am gay. Will you still love me?" The latter would be good.

Some of history's bravest martyrs were gay, not just the pioneering, American activist, Harvey Milk, but going further back into history—the Spartan King, Leonidas. He sacrificed himself at Thermopylae resisting the invading Persian forces in order to buy time for the Greek navy to regroup and successfully counterattack. (Not many people know that, in truth, "the 300

Spartans" were actually accompanied in battle by "the 700 Thespians" who, judging by the thespians I have met in my truncated career trading the boards, can only have added to the already abundant heroic man love.) And, of course, there was Federico Garcia Lorca, whose sexual courage and theatrical brilliance enraged the bestial Fascism of Spain's Nationalist (and Catholic) forces. Sadly, while revivals of his stage masterpiece, *Blood Wedding,* keep Lorca's name and legacy alive, Leonidas has to make do with Belgian chocolates.

Alas, the truth is more prosaic, Toby has rung because he has learnt of my state of ill health, but didn't want to just show up on my doorstep unannounced. One minute later, Toby walks in. Turns out he was phoning from my doorstep. Pavla kindly let him in for me and, of course Toby, about as gay as Dancehall DJ Bounty Killer and with an eye for the main chance, immediately started wanking up her with awful chat up lines like,
"What a beautiful accent…but then, you are a beautiful woman." "I hope London is treating you well…a woman like you deserves to be treated well." "You have so generously looked after my father…the least I can do is look after you."

Luckily, I was able to discreetly alert the perplexed Pole that Toby was simply using flattery in order to seduce her before flying back out of the country never to contact her again…until he next disembarks all horny at Heathrow. At this revelation, the frown fell from Pavla's face and she immediately arranged to see the rapacious rake that same afternoon for a meal and a movie. (I have since made a note of the above awful phrases for future reference.)

You already know that I am not one of those dads who believe in using their male offspring as guinea pigs to clone more advanced versions of themselves. Anyone who has heard Otis Ferry whistle, watched Liam Botham bowl, or read anything by Martin Amis, will know how futile that would be anyway. George Dubya and Baby Doc Duvalier, however, did do their fathers proud, I guess. (And I would be hard-pressed to choose whom I would rather be stuck in an overheated lift with—Ingrid Bergman or Isabella Rossellini.) Nevertheless, Toby has to be classed as the least successful of all my works, and that includes my early

National Youth Theatre competition entry, "An Arm and a Leg: the Thalidomide Musical!"

Since leaving Dulwich College (paid for by his mum) with a C in A Level Geography (and that's with the Head of Department admitting it is easier to pass Geography at A Level than it is to pass "Go" at Monopoly), Toby has tried, dealing in the city, despite not knowing the difference between fractions and percentages ("I use a calculator, Dad."); managing a restaurant, while convinced that Eggs Benedict is an order of monks ("It was a brasserie, Dad."); and selling yachts in a marina, when he can't even doggy paddle, let alone sail. What really infuriates me is that he has made money at all of them.

"Business is not about knowing things, Dad, it's about knowing people. I'm a relationship manager," he explained to me on Sunday. This from someone whose relationships last about as long as ceasefires in the Eastern Congo, and who seems to select his girlfriends in inverse proportion to their weight (I have yet to meet one that I couldn't fold up and carry under my arm like a collapsible umbrella.), at which point he tells me his current girlfriend (not his new date, Pavla, but some Californian heiress by the name of Brianna or Britney) is substantially heavier than her predecessors. I was about to venture that a medium-sized tattoo was enough to double the weight of his average paramour when Toby announces that Britannia, or whatever her name, is pregnant.

Not knowing what to do first, call up my soon-to-be-a-grandmother ex-wife, strike down my soon-to-be-a-father son, or warn off my soon-to-get-a-shag neighbor who has just returned from waxing her legs, Toby then takes advantage of my confusion, squeezes my shoulder, and murmurs in his idiotic mid-Atlantic twang, "It's the circle of life, Dad," before exiting, a still-unsuspecting Pavla waiting eagerly for him. I don't know what irked me the most—the casual disdain with which Toby announced this life-changing event, the lack of interest in discussing my life-ending event, or his quoting lyrics from *The Lion King* as his signoff line. I conclude, the last.

So, how should I feel now that I know upon my death I will be immediately replaced by my grandchild? Because, at the moment—and you may write me off as callous or blame my neurological doodah for messing with my frontal lobe's processing of emotion—but, truth be told, I feel nothing. Obviously, once I have met him/her/them (twins?) a few times and got to know (let's settle on the non-gender-specific personal pronoun) *it*, I expect to develop feelings *appropriate to its behavior*. Hopefully, they shall be of affection, but should the bugger turn out to be a bad'un, no amount of surname-sharing will get me onside. No Rose West/Sonia Sutcliffe/Primrose Shipman, Frau Rudolph Heydrich, "You gotta stand by them, they're family!" am I. That's why I can badmouth Toby without feeling parental guilt. "You are what you do," I say…and what Toby does is cock. In addition, I can't even guarantee that I will have even a surname in common with future progeny. I almost didn't with Toby.

Cressida, who was a child of the sixties, understandably abhorred patriarchy and wanted to call him not by my surname, Naylor, but by her surname, Parnell. "I see no reason why a child borne by its *mother* should go on to bear the name of its *father*?" she queried.

"Perhaps, but I see even less reason why it should bear the name of *your father*," I replied. "After all, the only reason your name is Parnell is because your father's was." This made Cressida cross and as a punishment I was forced to spend the weekend with her father. Gus—aka Lord Augustus William Penrose Parnell—was a landowning BUF Blackshirt who, before marrying Cressy's mother, was once the lover of Unity Mitford. Cressy insisted the old boy made that up to impress people. I said, "And someone who pretends to be the former lover of Fascist Oswald Mosley's Nazi sister-in-law is impressive how?"

Anyhow, eventually Cressy went with a double-barrelled name for Toby, even though I warned her that hyphenates, like similarly trendy carbon capture, simply store up trouble for the future. If we all, for the sake of gender equality, give our kids double-barrelled surnames so as to represent both their parents, then Toby Parnell-Naylor would currently be coupling with Briannon Jones-Smith and their son's surname would come out as Blah Parnell-Naylor-Jones-Smith who might couple with a girl called Blahette Sanchez-Olewayo-Konchesky-O'Connor to produce twins little Miss Parnell-Naylor-Jones-Smith-Sanchez-Olewayo-Konchesky-O'Connor and sibling Master Parnell-Naylor-Jones-Smith-Sanchez-Olewayo-Konchesky-O'Connor. Reading the register at school will take longer than the actual lessons and the backs of football shirts will have to be wider than the pitch. And don't expect me to send my great-grandchildren Christmas cards, because where am I going to find an envelope big enough to carry their surnames?

Mind you, better to be introduced with a very long name than by weight. I've not met a baby yet who wasn't introduced, "It's a boy, Alex, 8 lbs. and 6 oz.... or it's a girl, Tabitha, 6 lbs. and 11 oz.," as if the number of ounces will make any difference to how I feel about their birth. "Not sure if I like the sound of your new baby, a few grams on the heavy side." But, then again, as I proved above, it doesn't seem rational to have feelings toward someone you don't really know yet.

That was Sunday. I spent Monday to Friday failing to get Pavla to tell me what she and Toby were up to. Please, God, don't let him have made that girl pregnant too!

And double please, when my grandchild is born, don't let Toby repeat all the same mistakes with it that I stupidly made with him.

FC Naylor (175 lbs. and 10 oz.)

P.S. Tomorrow on Page 3, this paper will run an article about the nuclear submarine *HMS Profollia* having a bowling alley installed to deal simultaneously with sailor boredom and check that the sub is level in the water. Thought I'd let you know in advance it is our April Fool's Day spoof.

6. Saturday, April 7

My faith was challenged this week…not faith in God, to whom I feel no loyalty or attachment. I say that because many readers have falsely concluded that I am an atheist. My *socialism* and most recently my *suffering* are most often cited by armchair-theologians—surely *genuine* theologians being generally of intellectual rather than sporting disposition (*pace* Eric Liddle), are quite likely to be found in armchairs—and saloon-bar psychologists (see above) as reasons for my loss of faith. They are wrong. I acknowledge the possibility of God. As a rationalist, I do not find the hypothesis of an infinitely dense singularity (a concept along with "string theory" just as "ineffable", aka bollocks, as transubstantiation or the Holy Trinity), randomly exploding and starting the universe any more credible than that of an omnipotent, omniscient creator.

So, I do not have a problem with belief in God. I have a problem with worshipping him, and not merely because, as the universe's solo creator, he is responsible for childhood leukemia, hepatitis C, tsunamis, mustard gas, Hitler, AIDS, male pattern baldness, and Davina McCall, but because his main priority seems to be to require, in equal measure, two things—*adoration* and *obedience*. If there's one thing Catholics, Mormons, Shiites, Hassidics, and even the Amish all agree on, it is God must be both worshipped and have his will obeyed (even to the point—in the case of Abraham, the only prophet equally revered by Jews,

Muslims, and Christians—of stabbing an underage boy to death like some respect-hungry Hittite Hoodie). What sort of supreme, unequalled divinity remains so insecure, has such low self-esteem that it insists on pain of eternal damnation, on daily universal worship, and continuous complete obedience? If *I* were the most powerful entity in the universe, I wouldn't give a shit what ordinary people thought. In fact, *I* am one of the feeblest, non-entities in the universe, and I still don't care what people think of me. My advice to God is, "You created everything, well done…now don't be a beg-friend, move on."

No, my faith *in people* was rocked recently when Pavla arrived tearfully at my doorstep to announce that her employers had been burgled. Pavla who was in Regents Park having taken Eminem, i.e., my nickname for the over-fed, under-educated, two-headed monster that is Millimant and Mirabell, not Detroit's finest poet and rapper, to London Zoo, or as I like to refer to it in front of the little mites, *Animal Prison*.

Her employers, Hugo and Cassandra, were distraught at having their property invaded and the atmosphere was upsetting the little ones (don't care) and Pavla (do care), who felt she was being held responsible for the break-in because she only activated three out of the four locks on the front door. The fact that: 1) the key to the fourth is bent and useless, 2) just one of those Master Safe interlocking, high security, 5-pin tumbler, vertical action deadbolts is sufficient to make the place as hard to get into as Superman's Fortress of Solitude, but not quite as hard as the Garrick Club, and 3) the burglar actually got in through a rear window, did not seem to be factored into their judgement at all.

Realizing, however, this was not because the Montfords were a pair of overpaid, emotionally underdeveloped toffs, but because the traumatic nature of this all too often overlooked crime had impacted on their mental balance, I was forced to ring Adam and cancel that afternoon's much anticipated taking of my blood pressure and sped over to Primrose Hill with Pavla to see what I could do.

"An Englishman's home is his castle," I explained to the weeping Varsovian, "and when it is breached, it can make the owners feel very vulnerable and stressed. It isn't something you get over simply with time."

"I'm not from Warsaw, I'm from Krakow," she replied as if reading my thoughts or at the very least, my notes.

Shocked that no one had already been round before me to console the distressed family of owner-occupiers, who had not had to endure such a property loss since the erosion of feudalism in the late middle ages, I gathered the panicked householders together and put on my most reassuring voice—warm but also firm, like a Radio 4 weatherman.

"There, there," I said putting my arm round the shrunken shoulders of the erstwhile Master of the Universe, "never mind. Your wife's heavily insured Blackberry Curve and your Mac Power Book and Sony Hi-Res Camcorder may have gone, but the 50-inch Ferguson Plasma Screen is still attached to the wall, well six walls in total—get bored in the bathroom easily, do you? They didn't take your maroon twin Chesterfields, claw and ball Queen Anne chair, your set of eighteenth century brass Norfolk andirons, the pedigreed poodle/cocker spaniel hybrid, which I believe is now called a cockapoo, or your three-quarters of an acre of garden, and thank goodness they were disturbed before they had time to un-convert your loft; thankfully, it is still a six-bedroom, sun-magnet of an artist's studio and has not regressed to being a dusty, un-lagged, airless vault. Plus, you've still got your off street parking, driven once midlife-crisis classic, 988 Norton P43 Rotary motorbike, much coveted NW2 post code, and the top of the league Church of England Primary down the road in case the memory of what you describe as 'the symbolic rape of your family's nest' haunts you so badly you feel the need to sell and move south to Dulwich Village!"

Having stirred their hearts with my St. Crispin's Day motivational speech, I swept out of the violated building and into the street (nicking a silver and marble desk tidy on the way, just for the hell of it).

An embarrassed Pavla had to make her way home on her own half an hour later after apologizing for my behavior. Of course I have been forgiven; after all, if my brain disease isn't enough to affect my cognitive and emotional responses, my impending snuffing-it must be. Obviously, knowing you are going to die before getting to within five years of a free bus pass can be traumatic, too, though clearly not as much as being burgled.

Adam came around the next morning to take my blood pressure, which you may be interested to know after my tirade, is down!

FC Naylor

7. Saturday, April 14

Had a row with the editor this week. I made the mistake of popping in to see him and things got a bit out of hand. Things were not boding well when I finally came face to face with receptionist "Michael" and found a petite Asian beauty behind the desk, the spitting image of the Thai masseuse who gets it on with Emmanuelle in the movie of the same name. Cressy and I saw that together at the Prince Charles Cinema off Leicester Square back in 1974. It was the first sex film you didn't have to lie about seeing and we weren't the only couple there either. (I'd swear in court I saw a young Harriet Harman in the cinema that night, although her private secretary insists I dreamed this). Anyway, the girl, who was raised in Glasgow and not Bangkok, takes immediate offense even though I tried to explain it was actually quite a good film—thoughtful, stylish, from the woman's POV, erotic rather than dirty, adding that the butter scene in *Last Tango in Paris* was far more crude and tendentious than Just Jaekin's softcore romanticism…but this cinematic deconstruction only made matters worse.

Alistair comes prancing out of his office to find out what all the screaming is about (she started it) and reveals that this woman is not "Michael," who is off today, but an intern he appointed called Sonya. I immediately check that he is paying Sonya at least minimum wage—he's not—employers always take advantage of young people's enthusiasm about starting a career in the glamorous world of media and deliberately underpay these trainees, or interns, or whatever they call them. I instantly get her wages raised by 25 percent. Sonya is now more inclined to forgive what she wrongly perceives as my old-fashioned sexism and makes me a cup of Americano with extra espresso served with a smile. What a sweetie. I sip it triumphantly and finish by declaring that "exploitation" isn't confined to the movies. I briefly consider asking the sexy twenty-two year old out for dinner at The Thai Pavilion, but decide to cut my losses.

Despite this contretemps, Alistair surprises me by complimenting me on last week's column. Normally I have no respect for the hack's opinion—this is the man who once put Andrew Lloyd Webber on the cover of the annual Sunday Supplement, "Top Ten British Cultural Icons" edition, purely to get a backstage pass so he could meet Connie from *The Sound of Music.*

"Yes, FC." (That should have rung an alarm bell, calling me by my first name—well initials—instead of my surname.) "I think your references to your brain disease and high blood pressure are both courageous and touching, and readers' letters reflect this, too."

I said that was an aside, the article wasn't about my illness. The point of the piece was to highlight the contradiction between the principle of divine justice and the reality of being a random victim of crime.

"Really," he said. "When I read it, it didn't really seem to have any point."

"My brief was to write a f***ing diary, Alistair. Not every week in a person's life has a point, does it? If you want to know what a friend did last week you don't ask, 'So what was the point of last week, eh?' It's their *life*, not a soap opera!"

Anyway, Alistair must have scattered some feisty seeds in his herbal tea that day because he came back at me. "You sound just like your column, all preachy like an undergraduate essay."

I replied, "Really, you need to read some of your leader pages then; they're more GCSE citizenship presentations written by the Head of PE, which if you had ever been within one hundred meters of a state school, you might know what that meant. I'm not going to turn my column into a chronicle of sympathy-seeking symptom specification. There is more to me than my illness. If Stephen Hawking wrote a column for you, you wouldn't tell him, 'Oh, and Stephen, don't forget to remind the readers how awful it is to have that funny voice and no longer be able to run the 3000m steeplechase. Would you?'"

"No," Alistair confessed.

I continued. I was on a roll. "You wouldn't hire Duncan Goodhew merely to talk about what it's like not to have any eyebrows!"

"We would never hire Duncan Goodhew."

I conceded the point, but this combination of vigorous debate and caffeine made me a little too bouncy, and the coffee goes down the wrong way provoking a choking fit. Alistair is genuinely alarmed and he attempts to call Dr. Gupta, the paper's medical correspondent while ingeminating, "Are you alright, are you alright?"

I put him straight. "Of course, I'm alright. Why is it every time I cough everybody assumes I'm about to spit blood and keel over. Coughing doesn't always mean cancer or TB. What is it with everyone? Do you think at the theatre whenever someone is heard coughing during the quiet bits, the ushers think, *Oh, oh, another stiff to drag out of the stalls. Never mind, show must go on?*"

I blame Hollywood; every time a character over thirty is seen coughing in a film it is never a tickly throat or some coca cola that went down the wrong way. No, the next time you see them they have to be in bed all gaunt and pale trying to get in touch with the gay son they haven't spoken to in twenty years.

"Is your son gay?" asks Alistair. "You should write about that in your column!"

"No, he's not gay," I tell him. "He's just got his girlfriend *enceinte*. If you read the bloody column, you would know that."

One recently published columnist's lens was so inwardly focused that she went as far as writing an entire best-selling book about her son's mental illness. Her fellow journalist husband, not to be outdone, then wrote an article entirely about…his wife's book. I am now waiting to complete *la ronde*, for the son to write a book about his father's article. One word to this self-exposing family—*boundaries!*

"Like I have got time to read your column!" Alistair spits out.

"Then how do you know if it is all preachy and essay-like?"

I got him good and proper with that one and underlined this by rising to my feet, leaning over his desk, and swiping the piece of Lego off his beloved Richard Rogers diorama that represents his future premises. (I really hope I die before then. It looks not dissimilar to the dystopian space ship in the cartoon, *Wall E.*) I then flick the polycarbonate cuboid across the room and march out of his office with my shirt stained and smelling of roasted Arabica beans, but my pride intact and confidence sky high. This time I do ask out the radiant Oriental flower at reception, but she turns me down.

"I'm sorry," she says, "that is very flattering, but I am already dating an older man. Do you know Alistair's PA, Michael?"

I don't know what the point of this week's column is, but Alistair, if you are reading this, job done anyway.

FC Naylor (BP 135 [systolic], over 80 [diastolic])

8. Saturday, April 21

I am writing this in my underpants. No, I am not in Abu Ghraib or even Belmarsh being "conditioned" for interrogations that David Milliband insists never happened, and my physical position would more accurately be described by a physiotherapist or my concerned neighbor, Pavla (although we are currently not speaking to each other) as *hunched* rather than *stressed*. Nor, have I been stripped by robbers, fans, or the producer of the latest reality TV show, *The Sick in Their Smalls*.

The reason is my clothes are being cleaned by Pavla at the laundrette—she isn't speaking to me, but she still feels obliged to look after me. I am currently searching for the most appropriate place to lay the blame for my predicament and I have temporarily parked it at the door of *Medicine for Profit*. You might know that institution better as *Private Health Care*. In a typically "New Speak" way, those mercenaries who make a living auctioning scarce medical resources to the highest bidder, as opposed to the sickest, have hijacked the word "private" to conceal the shabby truth of what they really do. "Private" comes with positive connotations of individuality, choice, and personal freedom (okay, "Private" also used to be a chain of sex shops). *Selling* and *profit* conjure less an image of a beneficent physician following a life-long vocation to heal, than just another other c**t after your money. Anyway, I shall leave the ethics of the medical industry to another day and concentrate on how my trousers and favorite dress shirt got covered in stains.

Last Wednesday, Adam had me seen by a neurosurgeon friend of his—they play squash together at King's College Hospital's sports ground, Griffin's. They got chummy at the London Hospital Med School on account of Adam losing to him regularly.

I was once certain this was one of those lopsided friendships, like you see with some girls—the good-looking, confident one hanging out with a plain, fat friend to make herself feel even better...and also so when they meet a pairs of blokes, she will always end up with the cuter one. Then I realized that Adam, shrewder than I took him for, was playing the long game. Dr. Matthews, his friend, is a teaching hospital consultant who does private practice on the side and earns three times Adam's salary, plus he gets invited to lavish *conferences* in Miami, Marbella, and Marrakesh whenever some pharmaceutical company launches a new Alzheimer drug "whose side effects include high blood pressure, intestinal bleeding, impotence, acne...and rage." (Frankly, I'd rather forget all my past than remember such a present.) Adam never gets wined and dined. As a consequence, Matthews is now eighteen stone with high cholesterol and arrhythmia, and the effort required to win a squash match against Adam *now* would bring on immediate cardiac arrest.

Anyhow, Matthews has offered to give me a free FMRI scan and analyse the data himself to get a more reliable prognosis. I reluctantly accede to undergo these tests. Of course, Pavla finds out—essentially because I tell her—and promises to pray for good news.

I told her not to pray since she knows my feelings about religion. A lively discussion inevitably ensued in which a substantial amount of Battenberg cake gets thrown. I'd like to be able to say that she started it—she is a Catholic and you know how religious devotees can be quick to anger. As I pointed out to her, adding as proof that she need only ask the inhabitants of Manhattan or Kashmir, the relatives of Joan of Arc or any living Albigensian (if you can find one), or look up the history of Buganda where more people were killed by warring Protestant, Catholic, and Muslim factions in the late nineteenth century than in the entire previous history of that East African kingdom.

Pavla did not see how this had anything to do with her wishing to pray for me…and on reading what I have just written I have to say I'm not sure if I do either. Fortunately, tempers remained cool and tea continued to stay confined to our cups, even after I followed up by saying how presumptuous and what an invasion of privacy I think it is for Mormons from America to go around England digging up the parish records of every church and praying for the salvation of the long-since dead without their consent. She responded by pointing out it is impossible to seek permission from the dead and then asked what a Mormon was.

Dextrously sidestepping this diversion, I plunged relentlessly into my banks of evidence against the efficacy of prayer. It was at this stage I noticed the rhythm of our sipping had become disturbed, but I didn't have a clue quite what this presaged.

"To paraphrase Samuel Johnson, Pavla, 'Prayer is the last refuge of a scoundrel.'"

"Mr. Johnson, he does not visit you?" she asked innocently.

"Alas, soon I fear I shall be visiting him."

"Would you like me to drive you there? I can make a picnic."

I wanted to tell her that—as any Mormon worth his salt (lake city) would know—*Mr. Johnson* was one of the long-since dead, that he actually was taking about patriotism and not prayer, and we only have Boswell's word that he said anything of the sort in the first place. Apropos quoting quotations of other quoters, I also wanted to tell her that Mohammed was illiterate and the Koran was actually put in writing by his scribe, Zaid Ibn Thabit, after his death (plus Mohammed never claimed that God spoke to him, but rather the Archangel Gabriel passed on God's words to him). This means Mohammed would not have been able to read the transcription in order to check it, which means Zaid, a simple secretary as opposed to the infallible Last Prophet and Messenger of God, could have made mistakes or even stitched up the old fellow so the text that is being examined so scrupulously and fought over so passionately might, in fact, not be what it is held up to be!

However, I said no such thing. Instead, I told her how every American athlete who has ever won a race, when interviewed trackside invariably thanks first his coach and then God for making him win. And, isn't it arrogant to assume God will find the time to grant their prayers to win the World Student Games 400-meter hurdles when He clearly is too busy to answer those of the parents of Madeleine McCann. And, exactly why should He choose to answer one runner's prayer for victory and not that of his rivals, a dilemma particularly problematic at the quadrennial Pan American Games where all the competitors—*pace* the Cubans—are either U.S. Evangelical or Latin American Catholic.

By this stage, crumbs are tumbling out of my mouth like Palestinians from tunnels in Gaza and Pavla is stirring with unnecessary force.

"And, I can name at least four 100m world record holders who have failed drug tests, if you want," I add with a flourish.

"Please don't." She says. But, I do…and then some.

"Carl Lewis, Ben Johnson, Tim Montgomery, and Justin Gatlin amongst the men alone. There. And, if prayer was of any use, how do you explain what happened to the faithful in Sago Church, West Virginia after the local mine exploded a couple of years ago? They celebrated the sheriff's inaccurate announcement that all the town's thirteen miners had survived by thanking God for answering their prayer vigil, then received the corrected announcement that, in fact, only one had and the other twelve were dead."

Tea was now vaulting the edge of my cup and splashing into my saucer like panicked steerage class passengers on the Titanic, and the hapless Pavla quickly put away the uneaten remainder of our Lyons treat to give to her flatmates upstairs. But, although I had by now silenced her, I still hadn't finished.

"And *you* of all people should be the most sceptical about prayers being rewarded." She was almost out of the door, but that caught her attention.

"They were Polish, you know, the twenty-six Christians returning from their pilgrimage to Notre-Dame-de-la-Salette in the French Alps, only to die in a blaze when their coach driver misjudged a bend and drove off the road. Fickle is 'Our Lady,' eh? Maybe they did not leave enough in her collection plate."

At that stage, Pavla, patience snapping, turned and I ended up covered in buttercream, flour, and tea.

No, she didn't throw anything at me. She turned and said calmly, "You say these things because you are very frightened about taking this medical test. I will pray even harder." So *I* threw the tray at *her*, but the tablecloth got caught on my cufflink—my dress shirt does not come with buttons—and the whole she-bang avalanched on me like…well, like an avalanche.

FC Naylor

P.S. Results aren't back yet, but Matthews has put my name down for some new drug trial he has been bribed to promote. Figure it can't make things any worse.

9. Saturday, April 28

Pavla is not speaking to me because she claims that everything she says ends up in this column. Well, what Pavla doesn't know is that because of my diary, people are sending fan mail—to her.

Emails and letters headed with quotes like:

"How do you put up with him?"

"How are the twins getting on?"

"Have you thought of enrolling them on the Natural Child-Centred Holistic Multiple Birth Policy Action Development Programme Project Initiative blah wank blah…" or

"Co jesteście ty noszenie, Pavla?" (Which I am informed translates as, "What are you wearing?")

These, along with two job offers and a proposal of marriage. I, on the other hand….

So, who is gaining from this column? Certainly not me! Even Curry's Digital, from whom I bought my electronic goods on HP, got wind of my ruse through this column and a zealous chap in customer care called to demand them back, until I asked his supervisor if the High Street retail giant really wanted to sue a dying man over a bloody telly, to which he said, "Yes," they would. (Apparently low prices are the one thing totally immune to bad publicity.)

That's why no amount of personal stories about Bangladeshi orphans working eighteen-hour shifts in semi-darkness stitching duvet covers for fifty cents a day will ever close the doors of Save

Now or Easy Buy. I shall continue to boycott such goods, but then I still sleep in bedding bought before the industrialization of South Asia. I am of the firm belief that a sheet is for life, not just for Christmas.

Still, it got me thinking that over the years I really have accumulated some crap in the flat that should probably be put up for review. Maybe now is the time to do that—do a bit of purging, stop avoiding those tough decisions, sort out my priorities, and get some newfound clarity.

Therefore, I did my week's domestic duties: 1) Trip to minimarket for food, shop while cleaner paid for by column earnings does hoovering. (Well, the poly-cotton shirts iron themselves, I reckon.); 2) go through mail, i.e., chuck everything not handwritten into recycling bag; nothing printed in the mail ever improves quality of life; and 3) that's about it.

That left me the rest of the week (from 1:00 P.M. Monday) free to go through my stuff like an archaeologist excavating the dig of his own life.

Monday at 4:15 P.M., I stopped to watch *Countdown*. (I record it at 3:30, but prefer to watch it at its old time. When Jonathan Shaw MP raised this schedule change in Parliament, I almost renewed my membership of the Labour Party that I terminated after Tony Benn lost out to Denis Healey for the Deputy Leadership in '81.) Earmarked for oblivion were: 1) 2005 Official Queen's Park Ranger's Wall FC Calendar, and 2) nothing else.

And, by lunchtime, even the calendar had been reprieved. January 2008 was a "Legends" month with a montage of pictures of 180-goal striker Brian Bedford, 548-match player Tony Ingham, plus Phil Parkes, Rodney Marsh, Stan Bowles, Paul Parker, Ray Wilkins, and Sir Les. QPR being what it is, we only have enough legends to fill a calendar up to about August. However, our rubbish managers could fill a bloody encyclopedia, so I had to keep that one. The 2009 calendar I still need because it has everything I did last year written on it.

After creating even more chaos, I ultimately decide to keep everything. Why should I add to the stench and volume of a landfill or feed the hunger of a toxin-spewing incinerator? Besides, my things are *history*. Kids have no sense of history, no sense even of memory because they don't keep anything. Not real tangible artifacts. No books, magazines, newspaper cuttings, cards (except Yugioh), letters, posters, prints, LPs, videos, or journals. Everything is digital, provisional, temporary. The only indelible records in circulation now are the asinine tattoos that circle the navels, curl round the biceps, or hover above the arses of the young and the drunk. There is no correspondence to treasure and publish anymore, only the terse coded messages that are easily wiped from the memory of mobile phones and computers, from Facebook and from Twitter, as chalk is from a blackboard. Songs and TV programs are not preserved on tapes or discs to alphabetize, but downloaded onto tiny memory cards or hard drives, and then lost there or wiped away to make room for more ephemera. Shelves are empty, walls are bare, because art has been reduced to web content, literature to iPhone bits, and ideas have to be less than 140 characters long. Photographs do not adorn walls, but are trapped unseen inside pocket-sized silver boxes. No more breaking through stone walls or lifting dusty sarcophagi lids to uncover the mystery of history. Everything is invisible and private, or permanently exposed and shared in cyber space. Buildings will soon be entirely empty of things. Even the direction-guiding footprints, trails of desks, and cables are disappearing as everything goes portable, Nano and WiFi.

So, as inequality swells, nationally and globally there will be two types of home, but both will be empty—that of the poor who cannot afford to put anything in them and that of the rich who choose to put nothing in them, instead keeping everything they want in a single portable device that appears to store everything and link to everything, but is in reality no more than plastic and copper. These empty homes will be very bad for historians…and burglars.

So (after *Countdown*, in which I got the Conundrum the quickest and beat the sixteen-year-old Basingstoke prodigy by ten points: TRTAPCUOL = PLUTOCRAT), I decided to leave everything in my flat as it was.

Rooms should be messy because lives are messy. They don't conform to an ordered pattern or progress along straight paths.

The colors of my postcards from the North Italian lakes clash with the textures of the Bolivian bowler hat, the red floral curtains obscure the yellow pinned-up reminder notes, uneven piles of Pelican paperbacks are stacked on top of a pile of TV-themed board games, and Toby's first painting of me peers out from behind a black umbrella and 1987 E-K telephone directory. Clutter and disorder, coincidence and non sequitur are the discordant themes of my past. My living room is the museum of my life. Why should I reorganize my things to justify the teleological lie that life is a purposeful route through an ordered universe? I shall not.

Alistair says the real reason I shall not throw away any of my stuff is because I am indolent (posh Scots for *lazy bastard*), so I showed him the fading love note that I chanced across while unpinning various memorabilia from the cork board wall (specifically an old Private Eye cartoon of Rinka the dog from the Jeremy Thorpe trial). It was a yellowing, but very explicit *billet doux* from his current wife when she was still my wife, written in her own hand. And, stapled to the back was an even more explicit Polaroid of his wife using that hand. He quickly changed the subject.

FC Naylor

P.S. Pavla is back. She saw me rummaging around through the window, and became concerned. She feared that by sorting out my things I was settling my affairs in preparation for imminent death. I assure her I haven't got that far down the road, but I casually admit to being weary after my aborted spring cleaning, and she volunteers to tidy up!

10. Saturday, May 5

Following the success of *the issue about the issue of my issue,* today's column is a diary entry about diary entries viz., May 7, which, in two days time, will appear in diaries as May Day Public Holiday. Adam came round last week to see the latest cast-the-lead-in-a-west-end-musical contest. His wife forbids him from watching it in their house, but his children are at sleepovers and it is the final, so he has been given permission to come here. I don't follow the program on account of it being, well, shit I suppose is the word, but my money is on the one with the professional song-and-dance training winning. The same way that girl and boy with the song-and-dance training ended up winning the *Sound of Music* and *Joseph.* Of course, I might be totally misreading Lord Lloyd Webber, who might indeed be a risk-happy and charitable fellow happy to commit millions of pounds and a lifetime's reputation to the vagaries of the public vote and anoint some amateur chump (John Sargent?) to pilot his show to success or…I could be right and the chap with the training will win, especially now after that clip of his dying grandmother making her appeal. Although I swear the same woman made an appeal for a completely different family last year. She has to be a plant, either that or a very promiscuous *Land Girl* in the 40s.

Anyway, Adam is looking forward to the bank holiday, to which I replied,

"Isn't it ironic that May Day, a holiday celebrating the Labor movement should be called a *bank* holiday, especially when you consider the central role the banking industry has in maintaining the economic capitalist infrastructure? The Rothschilds would be appalled."

After shushing me and uttering something like, "He's going to do Curly's song from *Oklahoma*," Adam then declares that May Day Bank Holiday has nothing to do with the Labor movement and is a Pagan fertility festival. I had to spend four verses of *The Farmer and the Cowman* explaining the groundbreaking consequences of the May 1886 Haymarket Riots in Chicago, which led to the martyrdom of five innocent trade unionists, hanged after a rally in support of the eight-hour day got out of hand and a policeman was killed.

This doesn't stop Adam babbling on about maypoles, Walpurgis Night, and Celtic cults, to which I replied that being neither a Wiccan nor in a trade union, but rather a Jew, he should probably go to work on Monday.

Although few have much nostalgia for the now defunct annual parade of T-54s trundling through Red Square or ICBMs strapped to the backs of flatbed Gorky trucks being dragged past saluting Politburo septuagenarians in matching Astrakhan caps like a carnival float designed by Dr. Strangelove, the sacrifices of the working class to make this day possible must never be erased from history. To embrace that sacrifice I went to the pub to express my solidarity with the common man. I didn't have to…I embrace the common man whenever I get on the bus, enter a shop, or walk the street. Especially the street, where I frequently trip over the litter of the common man for which I blame the capitalist producers of the shiny colourful throw-away packaging in which they dress their wares like pimps adorning their hos in leather and lace. However, Adam was moaning about how I romanticize the mob, the *menu peuple*, while actually avoiding them. Of course, this is rubbish, but I went to the pub anyway largely to avoid the rest of *Evita and her Superstar Cat Express*. That proved impossible, however, because all the common men in the pub were watching it.

I tried to get the channel changed, but it only resulted in a fight. Emotions were already high (as a result of some Croydon teenager with a speech impediment having sung *One Day More* from *Les Misérables*), the place was packed and after my intervention, it turned ugly. A shame really, because all that passion combined with the camaraderie and the sheer density of people, if harnessed, could be a huge power for change. Chartism, the French Revolution, the fall of Ferdinand Marcos, and the demise of the Poll Tax were all triggered by numbers on the street. Although, temporarily, all united against me, the brawlers soon splintered like Trotskyites into sects, and a better tomorrow was postponed in favor of a punch up over the relative merits of Leona Lewis and Alexandra Burke. I returned to my flat (I told the mob I was dying and they left me alone, although some copper-haired mesomorph still wanted to have a go) to explain the origin of the pub riot to Adam.

"False consciousness, propagated by the commercial media as agents of the ideological superstructure that protects its capitalist economic base like a shell on a turtle, has once again divided the working class pushing it to turn violently in on itself."

"I thought BBC1, Naylor, wasn't a commercial media," Adam replied pedantically, ignoring my historical exegesis altogether.

I was about to explain Marcuse's theory of repressive tolerance with regard to state media in bourgeois democracies, but it was at this precise point that the lisping teenage Chav was declared the winner and Adam's attention was drawn elsewhere... Enjoy May Day.

FC Naylor

11. Saturday, May 12

On her way to Dulwich's Horniman Museum, that beguiling bastion of Imperial philanthropy, taxonomy, and condescending cultural curiosity that so consumed the leisure time of Victorian capitalists when they weren't being whipped by their corseted mistresses, Pavla dropped in with Millimant and Mirabel—don't ask me which is which. Generously offering up a rather delicious Lyons Lattice Treacle Tart and pot of Earl Grey, which might have been imported by Frederick Horniman's tea trading company itself, Pavla, despite having had to sneak under a rising Iron Curtain to reach these shores, has a stronger sense of our national legacy than the more Tiramisu, Ginseng, Tabouleh, Okra, Lassi, Sushi, and Amaretto-inclined metropolitans in our city. (If one consumes regularly all these foreign specialities *at home*, what culinary discoveries will remain to excite us when we go abroad?)

While at this palace of ethnography and zoology, I quickly experienced, up close, the contemporary phenomenon of negative attention seeking. When I was the father of a young child, feral growling while simultaneously punching your sibling and deliberately tipping over a milk jug was called "acting like a knob," but today it has acquired a pseudo-medical soubriquet. It is the same rebranding that occurred in the 1980s when "feeling too blue to go to work" was pathologized as chronic fatigue syndrome/myalgic encephalomyelitis, and in the 90s when "being very naughty" became attention-deficit hyperactivity disorder, a cough became asthma, and "being illiterate" became dyslexia. Consequently, today every spoilt little bugger who is a tad self-absorbed or anti-social has "an autistic spectrum disorder." This conveniently takes the parental upbringing out of the picture and shoves all the blame (no differently from when evil spirits and gypsy curses were the scapegoats for problem behavior) onto an abstract medical condition that, of course, can't answer back.

I should know. I was a very bad parent. And, is not cot death/sudden infant death syndrome a euphemism for murder? (*Editor's Note: This is neither the view of The Commentator, nor of any individual or body within, allied to, or subsidiary to Parnell Media Holdings or the Parnell Group PLC.*)

"I know what you mean, Pavla," I said later in my flat, firmly removing the tea set from Mirabell (or Millimant) while challenging him to close his angry little fist around my rather hot spoon. "I took a tilt at the television industry in last week's column," (Pavla no longer reads them for the sake of our friendship) "and I got three offers from TV companies yesterday alone. Does that make me guilty of negative attention seeking?"

I never found out Pavla's opinion, as she didn't hear my question on account of having to leap low to the left faster than Alan Knott to an Ian Chappell leg glance, in order to catch the plate of jammy dodgers that one of the Ms had attempted to drop onto the Arding and Hobbs acrylic rug that constitutes the only household good I hung onto after my divorce—and only then after finding it in a skip outside the Chelsea mews house into which Cressy and Toby moved.

After an ear bashing from Alistair about the need for cross-promotion, the Naylor brand, and then a confession that *LCD TV and Filmed Entertainment* was a recent acquisition of the Parnell empire and was looking for content, I agreed to follow up on one of the enquiries. (Alistair prattled on about the board at Parnell wanting us to go "multi-platform," whatever that means, and are majorly expanding into TV, web and mobile electronic media in partnership with some private equity fund blah blah blah.)

So, I was sent off to meet some chap called Brett Parfait, LCD's Director of Programmes. Parfait seemed to anticipate my scepticism about the project—either because of my reputation or because my opening words were, "I am very sceptical about this project." To be honest, the deciding factor that led to our meeting was not helping out my editor, nor my ex-wife, but the fact the headquarters of LCD (the acronym was never explained, but I presume it stands for *Liquid Crystal Diode* rather than *Lowest Common Denominator* on the basis that today's media type wouldn't know the difference between Lord Reith and Lord's Cricket Ground, or Ken Loach and Ken Barlow, let alone the difference between a denominator and a numerator) have an excellent view over the canal at Little Venice where Cressida and I used to buy marijuana from an American jazz drummer in the seventies. (*Editor's Note: Endorsing the past or present misuse of Class C drugs is neither the view of The Commentator, nor of any individual or body within, allied to, or subsidiary to Parnell Media Holdings or the Parnell Group PLC.*)

"Don't worry, FC—can I call you FC? At LCD we're not interested in making shit like Endemol and RDF. (*Editor's Note: The contention that Endemol and RDF make 'shit' is neither the view of The Commentator, nor of any individual or body within, allied to, or subsidiary to Parnell Media Holdings or the Parnell Group PLC including LCD Television and Filmed Media.*) What we *are* interested in is quality television, landmark television..."

I interrupted, "I want to present a series of hour-long documentaries on pioneering twentieth-century artists and thinkers starting with Bertold Brecht, Diego Rivera, and E. P. Thompson." Brett didn't even a catch breath at this announcement. He had either read my mind *or* the covers of the biographies I had under my arm of Bertold Brecht, Diego Rivera, and E. P. Thompson...

Then Brett interrupted me. "I want you to present the life of a different man also best known by his initials. You."

"U Thant?" I said, misunderstanding the homophone. "The Burmese Secretary General of the United Nations? Why?" By the way 'U' is not strictly an initial, it's an honorific equivalent to "Mister" in Burmese. People seem to get initials and acronyms muddled up all the time. For instance, it is nonsense to talk about the "the HIV virus." There is no HIV virus, and I don't mean that in the way the former South African Minister of Health, Manto Tshabalala-Msimang meant it. It's the *HI Virus*. "HIV" stands for **H**uman **I**mmunodeficiency **V**irus. "HIV virus" then becomes "**H**uman **I**mmunodeficiency **V**irus *virus*." There is no such thing as a PIN number either. "PIN" stands for **P**ersonal **I**dentification **N**umber. "PIN number" is "Personal Identification Number *number!*"

Brett smiled at me. "Not U Thant. You, FC."

"UFC? The Ultimate Fighting Championship; don't they already have their own show on Bravo?"

"No." His cool was evaporated by now. "I want *you* to front a series about the life of yourself, FC Naylor!"

I thought we were going to continue with a routine based on misunderstanding to compare with Groucho and Chico's "Party of the First Part" in *Night at the Opera* or Abbott and Costello's "Who's on First?" in *The Naughty Nineties* (incidentally, written not *by* Abbott and Costello, but *for* them by Michael Musto for a measly $15), but suddenly we understood each other. Or, rather, I understood him. He didn't want to make a series about my *life*, offering a reappraisal of my work in the context of historical shifts in the paradigm of theatrical aesthetics and literary theory…but a series about my death. It would be a landmark because it would be the first to show the subject of a documentary breathing his last breath, live on camera.

Brett explained, "ITV talked of doing that in the Malcolm and Barbara show about the guy with Alzheimer's, but they got chicken and stopped turning the camera shortly before he died. LCD doesn't get chicken."

"No, that would be KFC."

I said no to this grisly spectacle, but Brett said he would still love to work with me if I come up with any other *landmark* ideas. It turns out LCD actually stands for *Landmark Content Devisors* and their USP is producing stuff that has never been done before on TV. I essayed that none of my plays had been on TV.

"What about making my satire on contemporary idolatry, *Whore,* about the 1981 Royal Wedding? You could broadcast it on the anniversary of Diana's death. Or, better still, you could make a TV version of my swan song; it would be a last hurrah—

like *The Tempest*. That would be literally a first. My last script never even made it to the stage."

He didn't commit, but invited me to return with any novel ideas I might have, the following week. Next week I start my drug trial so the pain of such a task should mask that of needles being stuck in me. Now, back to Bravo and some mixed martial arts. If it's good enough for Roland Barthes, wrestling's good enough for me.

FC Naylor

12. Saturday, May 19

My errant son, "Toby," left a message on my answer phone last weekend. I don't hear from him for six months and now it's twice in six weeks, ah, the allure of being a published writer. Published weekly, in fact.

This is a rare privilege given that some truly great debut authors wilfully blocked out the public clamor for more masterpieces, never writing a second novel to cash in on the popular and critical success of their first. J. D. Salinger wrote the legendary *Catcher in the Rye* then no more novels, only a handful of short stories. Margaret Mitchell wrote the record-busting *Gone with the Wind* and nothing else. Harper Lee, the timeless classic *To Kill a Mockingbird,* and then not another word. Prince Charles gave us *The Old Man of Lochnaga*, and then starved the literary world of a follow-up.

On the other hand, how must others such as Donna Tartt and Irvine Welsh, in the same way that car crash victims and the unwittingly pregnant curse that foolish final extra shot they agreed to, regret the lack of restraint that spoiled what should have been a perfect weekend with hangover headaches like *The Little Friend* and *Filth*. (I was going to put Jeffrey Archer and Martin Amis in this category, but their first books were already rubbish, so they don't count.)

However, I had no time to find out what my prodigal had wanted, since Adam arrived soon after to take me to the Ansdell

Goodrich Laboratories in Esher, where I was about to be a guinea pig for a pharmaceutical company looking for its next blockbuster drug. Curse the expiration of those patents that allow generic copies to increase access to good health for the international poor. Voltaire's HD is rarer than obesity in Hollywood, so there is little chance of much return if this little druggy goes to market. However, the advanced stage of my condition shares symptoms with the increasingly popular killer—the stroke (aka cerebrovascular accident).

I wave to Pavla, who is at her window looking earnest and clutching rosary beads, upon which I shall not comment, and commence my first 48 hours away from home since I was arrested during the *Stop the War* march in 2003. (I wasn't actually held overnight in a cell, but adopted by a group of zealous fine arts students from Sussex University, who insisted on taking me to their digs in Brighton for the weekend to tell them stories about the golden age of CND and the legendary Aldermaston March of 1958. Not wanting to let them down, I recounted tales of MI5 informers, angry farmers setting fire to our tents, and an LSD-initiated love-in involving myself, a very well known folk band, and six Quakers—all of which I made up because I was actually Nine at the time and much more interested in discussing the pros and cons of Nat Lofthouse's second goal in the FA cup final against Man Utd with my dad, than banning the bomb.)

The drug trial, I am afraid, turned out to be considerably less exciting than Michael Crichton's *Coma* or the closing scenes of *Clockwork Orange* and mainly involved undergoing a bunch of boring tests, giving blood, being weighed, having my pressure taken, and my head x-rayed. I've had all that done at the dentist. I was hoping to have a CAT scan or MRI and climb inside one of those blue torpedo tubes, but I was told that would not be necessary. Then I took this drug or a placebo—one is not allowed to be told which—although I told Adam it better *not be* a placebo. I can stay at home to eat Smarties if I want.

I'm not allowed out for forty-eight hours in case a side effect registers.

The walls of the clinic are all different shades of green (which is considered calming, while blue is cold, and red leads to fights).

My fellow trialists are of all colors. Half are healthy and young, here for the money; the other half are sick, having had strokes. Their symptoms vary from slightly slurred speech or awkward movements to semi-paralysis. Nonetheless, all share a desire not to engage in conversation with me and watch TV instead (the very young use MP3 players). I normally prefer reading to telly (apart from my daily appointment with Jeff and Rachel), but my close eyesight is not as reliable as it was—blurred vision and mild headaches are what launched me into the testing program that uncovered my VHD. Therefore, I join the others in the TV room. It doubles as research so that by the time I leave I will have some great proposals to take to Brett at LCD. This is a rare twin-events week, hence the extra word count!)

When I do make my return to Little Venice, before I can get any words in, Brett has a proposal for me. He has gotten wind of my visit to the Lab and wants the cameras to follow me there—not as a case study in my physical decline, but as an insight into the interface between man and medicine. I tell him I think there is a great story in there and immediately outline for him all the personalities and events from the Lab—the absent doctors who have allowed a vindictive and officious nurse to rule over us like a Chechen warlord, the young kid driven by neglect and humiliation to a bloody suicide in the toilets, my instigation of a rebellion against the nurse's despotism, her lobotomizing of me, and finally the giant Red Indian who makes his escape after pitching a sink through a window. Brett, who can't believe his luck stumbling across such a rich real life drama, is still excitedly spell checking the word "lobotomize" before I reveal to him that this is actually the plot of *One Flew over the Cuckoo's Nest*. W****r!

"Good one, FC," he answers recovering composure as quickly as you would expect someone born without any sense of shame, taste, or judgment—qualities, it would appear inessential, if not downright burdensome, for those born into privilege then steered into television. "Does that mean you don't have any proposals of your own, FC?"

"*Au contraire*," I say and pitch him the results of my research. "I've deliberately skewed my proposals toward a younger demographic, mortgage-free with high disposable incomes to attract consumer product advertisers and with the thrill-seeking, open-mindedness attracted to the Landmark brand's innovative house style." Brett looks as if he is about to come. I continue.

"*Rape TV,*" I propose. "Could be a single program, a series…why it could be a whole channel. Sod filming police car chases, drunken brawls, or drive-by aftermaths, this is cutting edge reality television. If the women won't sign release forms, we can pixelate their faces. I'm sure they will sign, because we are going to be the first program to pay members of the public repeat fees rather than rip them off with lousy buyouts. When you consider only 5 percent of reported rape cases end in conviction and what women have to go through to get there such as invasive medical tests and intrusive cross-examination, at least this TV program will give them some financial compensation and won't judge their character. But, if you like *invasive,* then my second choice, *Strip Search: Heathrow,* says it all. Add *Strip Search: Prestwick, Luton,* and *Stanstead* and you have a franchise. Prefer celebrities to members of the public? Then *Pound of Flesh* has it all. A medieval castle set, instead of the usual island, jungle, or modern house and a Shakespeare theme to get that blacktop tabloid snob approval. Each of the castle mates is served a slice of meat and they have to guess which of the celebrities already voted out it belongs to."

"Belongs to as in *owned by*?" Brett asks.

"Where are your *cojones*? 'Belongs to' as in belongs to. We're not going to kill anyone—we're talking about celebrities with agents, after all, not members of the public. People would notice if their favorite skating chef or a waltzing cricketer disappeared. We're going to cook a piece of them instead. Just a little piece taken from the celebrity's buttock or thigh. I mean most of these people would pay to have that done anyway. We can call it *The Merchant of Venice* round! Alternative title—Come Dine on Me."

Brett is equivocal.

"Want to really make landmark television? Then make *Barabbas.* Twelve criminals all convicted of multiple murders; you give them a bunch of games to play, some booze to drink, and every week the public votes one back into jail to stay in prison forever. The murderer who is the winner at the end is given his freedom, just like...*Barabbas*. Think about it."

With a flourish I left the office, took a stroll down the towpath like Cress and I did when she was pregnant with Toby and couldn't sleep, and then I waited for a reply. Alas, all my proposals were rejected: 1) the *Rape* idea due to "the technical challenges of where to place the camera," 2) the *Celebrity Cannibal* idea because the Shakespeare theme was considered "too literary high brow and might alienate LCD's core demographic," and 3) the releasing of an unrepentant murderer into our midst was nixed because of "budget constraints," although we are considering offering it to foreign markets where they have capital punishment and ratings for the live execution of evictees would defray the costs of the show's security implications.

Incidentally, so far, I have not suffered any side effects to the experimental drug so the dosage can be increased and we shall see if it makes any difference.

Toby has rung yet again. He tells me he is in town with his pregnant girlfriend and he would like to bring her round to meet me. He also said that he read my column on the web last week and wanted to correct me. Toby emphasizes he never ever considered me *a bad dad*. He remembers me not being around much, that's all. Whether that means he *liked* me being absent, and that is what qualifies me as being *not bad*, is unclear. I shall find out what this is all leading to when he turns up.

FC Naylor

P.S. I posted Brett one last idea—a fly-on-the-wall documentary about pedophile vicars I call "Hot Under the Collar."

13. Saturday, May 26

Got my name in the *Media Guardian* for the first time on Monday. My TV program ideas instigated a furious exchange of letters between program developers, academics, journalists, and civil servants about "audience-driven television" versus "elite agenda-setting." The loudest voice celebrating give-them-what-they-want-television as heralding the birth of democracy in the media and condemning the application of "standards of quality" as cultural fascism was ironically that of the chief executive of a multinational media company educated at Eton and Cambridge. His market-led philosophical ideology (more Forrest Gump than Noam Chomsky) by analogy would give the seal of approval to the sale of Manhattan Island to Dutch explorer Peter Minuit because, after all, those Canarsee Indians *really wanted* those beads.

Anyway, I shall not return to the subject, but shall content myself with having provided the apple and thus been the green-grocer/midwife that facilitated this Olympian civil war of aesthetics, *midwife* being a serendipitous link to the next event to cross my calendar.

I agreed to meet Toby—after some prompting by Cressida (or rather her PA)—and with some trepidation, allowed him the opportunity to introduce to me his new (and pregnant) girl-friend. He wants to meet at Le Meriden in Piccadilly where tra-ditional English tea is served by East European waiters, accompanied by an East Asian harpist, to American tourists in a

French-owned hotel. I approve of the venue as accurately reflecting London's unique cosmopolitan identity, but this seems to undermine rather than bolster Toby's choice, as he wants his lady friend to savor an authentic English experience. I tell him that I will try to find out where Beatrix Potter and Colonel Mustard take tea together or, better still, chat about the weather while participating in an orderly queue outside the post office. Eventually, Toby agrees to meet across the road from Le Meriden at the café inside Waterstone's, Britain's biggest bookshop, in which, in line with the current New Age of Illiteracy, there should be plenty of spare room. I ask Pavla to come with me, not because I fear running out of things to say to my son and she is the same age as him, but because she has just been paid and I am a bit strapped for cash.

I regret this the minute we sit down opposite Toby and Lilah (?)—she's not called *Brighton* after all and she's bulkier than his previous consorts, i.e., she casts a shadow. Anyone looking at us is bound to conclude we are on a double date and that I am another of those venal old gits who has taken a second wife who is the same age as his son. However, just as I change my mind and decide I am not opposed to the idea of being mistaken for a man who could at Sixty One still attract a woman thirty years younger, I realize there is no one else here to see us.

Anyway, my thoughts are quickly steered elsewhere when Toby pulls out a fuzzy Polaroid photograph, and thrusts it in my face. I have to confess the first place my thoughts are steered to is the land of guilt and panic as I ponder what it is I have done that is so terrible that my own son is trying to blackmail me, probably to fund this new child he is going to have. Then my thoughts go to a second place, one of puzzlement and incredulity, since I can't remember having had the opportunity to do anything blackmail-able since the Brixton Riots of 1981 and surely there is a statute of limitations on criminal damage to a police helmet that wasn't even being worn by a policeman at the time. Then, just to be on the safe side—memory can be a tricky thing when you have VHD—I grab the photo and instinctively shout, "That's not me!" Pavla raises me from my reveries by throwing her arms around me and shouting, "Oh, he looks just like you."

"Well, I may have lost some hair and stoop a bit, but…" however, my objections are drowned out by Pavla cooing and I conclude this could never have been a double date even if we intended it to be, as I am reminded there are five people around the table not four, and this ultrasound photograph from the hospital is a picture of the fifth.

We relocate to the Marquis of Granby around the corner and swap Earl Grey and lemon drizzle cake for pale ale and pork scratchings—that's my England. I am about to tell the American girl she will need to live off more than the single olive in her Martini if she is going to successfully carry my grandchild to term when Pavla seems to anticipate my thoughts and launches into a series of hugs, kisses, and congratulations easily sufficient for the two of us; which is just as well since I am not over-keen on cuddling in public and am no longer certain if the future mother of my first grandchild is called Lilah after all. In fact, I am pretty sure that she is not. In fact, I fear it might be Luanne or Lianne, but settle on Lilah as a compromise between the two, a compromise, which like all compromises, ends up pleasing no one. Toby seems to want me to say something significant at this point, but all I can think of is the day Cressy confirmed she was pregnant with him and the mixed feelings I was foolishly unable to hide.

Children are wonderful. Of course, they are not *miracles* or *gifts from God*, but they are unique opportunities for a world gone bad to be put right. Of course, French structuralists like Louis Althusser will tell you that all individuals are prisoners of the historical social conditions into which they are born and over which they have no control. However, most structuralists are mad. Althusser hated his mother for loving his uncle more than his father, and ended up strangling his wife, so I don't think we'll be visiting *him* for advice on how to raise children. And, Michel Foucault was a homosexual, sadomasochist who approved of consensual sex between adults and children; so without being judgmental, let's just say that he had…issues. I wanted to bring up Lacan and Derrida, but Pavla interrupted me and said, " FC, tell us about that later; we want to hear what you said to Toby's mum when she told you she was pregnant." But *that was* what I said to

Cressida when she told me she was pregnant. Anyway, I did my fatherly duty and gave the lad the following advice.

"There are more children on earth than the earth can sustain," I said. "So, young man, you better be bringing one into it for the right reasons. This isn't about getting your Green Card, is it?"

Toby assured me it was not. "We're not even sure if we are going to get married."

I could see how that disappointed Pavla, but she is too nice to show it. I am not too nice to show what I think, so the next question was to Lily Sue.

"This isn't about my son's money, is it?" I asked.

(You see, Alistair has never fired on all cylinders—sorry, matey—but it is the third worst kept secret at the paper after the sports editor's hair transplant and the affair Sally the Deputy Head of Classifieds had with her Dutch male PA Koen and with Gail the female Security Guard on the back gate; bet you didn't know about that last one, did you?) Plus, Cressida is post-menopausal, so the chances are that Toby will inherit the lot on his own.

"Dad, Mary's (Of course, *Mary*, that's her name!) family owns half of Rhode Island; she has plenty of money."

Mary shuffled sideways so I could see her from behind her cocktail stick. "Well, she obviously doesn't spend it on food." Pavla dug her heel into my left foot, but I was so cramped under the pub table that it had gone to sleep and it barely registered. "I read that anorexics sometimes choose to get pregnant because psychologically it gives them permission to eat," I explained.

"Dad, anorexics can't get pregnant because their periods stop."

"Oh," I replied, "it must have been fat people then."

Then unexpectedly, like an assassin's arrow through the night, a cloudless dawn in February, a *mea culpa* from Arsene Wenger, or a tune you can't get out of your head from Stockhausen, Mary finally spoke. "Our baby's been created out of love, just like Toby was," and she held my son's hand.

Of course, Pavla started crying and blessing everyone, and thankfully it was time to leave, though Toby rang me later to say how much Mary liked me. Her honed New England good manners, I expect—Mary knows I don't have long to go. Then to my complete surprise, Toby added that the scan showed the baby was a boy and would I give them permission to name him after me. "Of course," I replied, "that's very flattering."

"Only thing is, Dad," added Toby, "you never told me what FC stands for."

Actually, I have never told anyone, not even Adam or Cressy (I distracted her with a poisonous fart when the Registrar read my full name out at our wedding. She was hallucinating on mushrooms in any case. However, I promised Toby that when the time came, before I go and the baby arrives—keeps the population static, very Green—I would let him know.

FC Naylor

14. Saturday, June 4

My mailbag has been full this week, or it would be if people actually sent mail. Let us say that communications have been abundant since last week's column and, unlike the stars of screen and print who have hate mail filtered out by a posse of loyal secretaries, and death threats channelled to the police, I receive the whole unadulterated lot. I must be honest, though. I didn't read any of it. I am under as much obligation to read your correspondence as you are to read this column, but the gist of it, I have on good authority (the switchboard operators at *The Commentator*), is that I have been under fire after my remarks about Michel Foucault. Has the *Rive Gauche* finally rediscovered its collective voice after the passing of Sartre, de Beauvoir, and Yves Montand? Are the students out on the streets of Paris in defense of the iconoclastic intellectual? No, most of the messages came from Manchester and London.

I have been accused by members of the Gay community of claiming that homosexuals should not have children (Manchester) and by the BDSM community (London and Home Counties) that fetishists should not either. Dubbed a socialist class warrior and living on the margins, I have never been particularly popular with feminists, lesbians, gay men, people of color, the disabled, or travellers. Apart from the mid-eighties, when Thatcher's millenarian stampede trampled pretty much every plant in the moral garden, heaving every conceivable outcast into an unlikely alliance that made Churchill and Stalin look like Richard and Judy (one rally on Blackheath Common had lined up on the podium everyone from *Baptists against the Bomb* to *All Men Are Rapists*, *Burn da Babylon Irie* to *Save Shropshire's Hedgerow Birds*, and saw Peter Tatchell arm in arm with the Regional Convenor of the Prison Officers Association). Oppressed interest groups, like shoppers at a sale, tend to see in each other not commonality, but competition for the best view from the moral high ground or the juiciest scrap from the establishment's table.

I don't care what class or gender, race or lifestyle group you hale from, you may have your baby with my complete indifference, provided you are prepared to look after it. You may adopt the unwanted, married or not, single or not. And, if due to problems of infertility a woman would like placed in her womb the egg of a stranger fertilized by the sperm of another stranger, by all means go ahead. In addition, if after the embryo matures and a baby is delivered then she and her partner (whether male or female) may even pretend to their friends and to each other that they are the parents of this child, when strictly they are respectively its human wrapping paper and human wrapping paper's best friend, I am not going to chide you. If make-believe is necessary to make you happy…

You see, it isn't the carriers I have a problem with, it's the donors. It simply doesn't feel right to give seeds or eggs and then scarper abandoning your subsequent offspring like a terrorist does a ticking bomb, murmuring to yourself, "I'm sure it will end up in good home." That's the dump and walk away attitude that makes it impossible to find kerb space to park in anywhere along Dog Kennel Hill on account of all the deserted rusting hulks with expired tax discs and owners blaming the plunging price of scrap metal for their misdemeanors. And, if it is bad for cars who can't cry themselves to sleep puzzling why their registered keepers walked out on them, think what it will be like for human children who will want an answer as to why their parents made them and then fled before even meeting them ("knock *up* ginger," rather than "knock down"). "It wasn't you, it was me," the deadbeat donors will confess to their former sprogs. "Too right," they will agree, "how could it have been me when you never even hung around to meet me." As for the anonymous donors or lying "parents" who withhold from the children their true parentage, I have two words for you…"**** ***" followed by another two, "Oedipus Rex." Sod's Law says if you don't know who your real parents are you are doomed to, at best, unknowingly murder your father and sleep with your sibling. At worst, should you be into MILFs…?

I have not been the best father. When Cressida and I separated, I did not fight for custody of little Che (as he then was) for several reasons: 1) I was still processing my emotions as a result of my split with his mother, 2) I was grappling with a career that seemed to be relentlessly slipping away from me, and 3) I was preoccupied with winning a political war on behalf of all our children, not just mine.

Oh, and there was another reason too…was it because I could not bring myself to take him away from his loving mother (for whom I still had feelings), especially with the knowledge that she was bound to do a better job of raising him than I ever could? No. It was that I didn't want to bring up the mewling bastard! They cost money, they take up space, they wake you up, and they stop you going out, on holiday, or to a party. You can't go chasing women and stay at their place on a whim or bring them back to yours (unless they are weird). You can't get drunk with your mates or high on your own, achieve your potential at work, stay up late, or watch an hour of TV uninterrupted. And they never, ever, ever go away! You have to take them to the shops and to the park; it takes so long to get them ready to go out you are often due back before you even leave. They shit, cry, vomit, and can't even talk for the first two years and then all they are interested in is saying what they want, never asking what *you* want! You have to buy them things and they keep getting sick, but are rubbish at explaining why, they break things, grow out of things, and you never stop worrying about them even when they grow up in case they get pregnant or AIDS or, God forbid, come home! Soon being held overnight by the police in a cell is no longer your nightmare, but your dream! Any bloke who tells you those are *not* the reasons he walked out and mumbles something about how he knew that if he stayed he "would only make things worse" and how you were "really better off without him," but he is different now and he really wants to "make up for lost time and be a part of his son's life"—now that he is in the England Under-21s squad and loaded—oh, and by the way, any chance of a shag for old time's sake since his current wife doesn't understand him the way you did...is a f***ing liar.

So, don't have them unless you really want them. Don't do it to make your wife happy because in the end, you won't. Don't do it because your mates are doing it because they aren't going to look after him, you are. Don't do it because you are getting old and you really should while you still can. Don't do it to please your parents, to fill an emptiness in your life, because you are bored, unemployed, unqualified, and desperately want respect, to be loved, a reason to get up in the morning, or because...why not? And never do it to leave a legacy because there are other ways—plant a tree, pay for a seat in a theatre with your name on the back, teach, or write. If you are Francois Mitterand, leave behind a pyramid in Paris; if you are Tony Blair, a Dome in London; or, if you are George Bush, a giant lifeless crater in the capital city of Mesopotamia, the cradle of civilization. But, not a baby unloved, abandoned, or given away.

So I've been mulling over that this week and hoping Toby takes heed better than I did.

I also got a phone message from Samuel French's Theatre Bookshop, which I didn't return. (I still have a copy of *The Iceman Cometh* with which, it is *possible*, that I absentmindedly walked out without paying for.) Anyway, actually they would like it back, but the main reason they called is someone has been trying to track down my last play, which I wrote in 1984 soon after Toby was born. I must have mentioned it in this column, I suppose. They don't have it in stock because it was never published, though I still have the manuscript somewhere. I'm not sure I would want it produced now, though, not after seeing Stanley Kubrick's *Eyes Wide Shut* on Channel 4. It was enough to make his fans wish the great man had died sooner. Nice to see Nicole Kidman take her kit off, though. If she had done it in *Bewitched* or *The Hours*, maybe I wouldn't have slept through the first or been transfixed by that basilisk nose throughout the second.

FC Naylor

15. Saturday June 11

An empty mailbag this week. Scores of complaints were sent from lesbian couples, gay couples, childless couples, single mothers, surrogate mothers, impotent men, barren women, career women, forty-, fifty-, and sixty-something *primigravida*, the HFEA, private sperm banks, Madonna, and Angelina Jolie. I ignored them all on the grounds that if children are so important to them, shouldn't they be looking after them instead of using up all this potential *quality time* badgering me? Actually, I did reply to Angelina Jolie (never fancied Madonna, looks like a weasel from *Toad of Toad Hall*), though my ironic and flirty tone seems to have been taken the wrong way and I am now the subject of a restraining order. Not that I am likely ever to find myself within 200 meters of Beverly Hills or Namibia, in any case.

I did get messages of support from The Society for the Protection of the Unborn Child, Opus Dei, and the South East London Nazi Party, which to me is about as useful as a job reference from Lehman Brothers. Funny people those "right-to-lifers"…despite their name they invariably support capital punishment, in some cases dispensing it personally via semi-automatic rifles from behind the bushes outside family planning clinics. I simply can't navigate my way through the paradox of the rights of the "unborn child." They claim an "unborn child" has the same rights as a "born child" on the grounds that it is only a matter of time before the former inevitably develops into the latter. However, by this logic "living people," or, to mirror their vocabulary, "undead corpses" get exactly the same rights as the dead, i.e., no rights at all, in which case we should all be climbing into coffins or jumping on pyres right now. (This might appear tangential, but if they do have souls as "pro-lifers" claim, then, when aborted fetuses go to heaven, do they have to live in jars? I don't want to appear selfish, but I would find that off-putting and surely heaven is a place where one should expect not to be made to feel uncomfortable all the time.

While we are on the subject, when you get to heaven, do you stay at the age at which you died? In which case the only difference between it and a Florida golf course would be that the overwhelmingly geriatric community of aged Westerners where life expectancy is sky high, would share space with millions of African toddlers where infant mortality rates are even higher. That is not a recipe for social cohesion, never mind the potential conflict between both age groups over the nappy-changing facilities. In addition, the implications of underage Muslim martyrs arriving to claim their promised virgin rewards are simply too problematic to pursue. (If, on the other hand, qualifying for heaven includes the privilege of choosing at which age you spend eternity, the place will be like one vast Glastonbury Festival full of Tweeting twenty year olds.) Anyhow, I tipped the whole lot into the recycling container. Mailbag empty.

In any case, I didn't have time to go through all my correspondence this week because I got a call from Dr. Matthews' secretary summoning me back to the lab at Ansdell Goodrich. When Adam showed up to accompany me, I inferred it was not to hear good news. Turned out one of the other trialists has developed side effects and a second has died, so everybody has been called back early.

"Well he was terminally ill, of course he died." I said sanguinely to my old friend.

"I suppose it might simply have been his time, but they want to be sure that this new drug treatment at the very least didn't hasten his death," Adam opined. (A case of markedly low ambition on the part of the drug company, if you ask me. What exactly is its mission statement? "To be global leaders in not killing our customers, by 2012?")

"Then there's that other patient who has developed side effects," Adam added.

"So hastening death isn't considered a side effect?" I retorted. "If the packet said, 'May cause drowsiness. Do not use heavy machinery. Also may hasten death,' I would call that a big f***ing side effect. And while you're at it, 'Cause of death might simply have been his time,' doesn't sound very scientific either. That conclusion is not going to get you a job as a coroner, is it, Quincy?"

"Quincy was a pathologist, FC. Very few coroners are qualified medics; in fact, they're more likely to be lawyers."

"I'm beginning to doubt that you are a qualified anything. Mystic Meg could make the same diagnosis as you for the price of a premium rate phone call and without putting me under the care of Dr. Frankenfurter whose cocked-up lethal experiments are beginning to make Porton Down look like Club Med."

I was about to go on when Matthews came in and interrupted. After a quarter of an hour sternly warning me that the contract I signed at the start of the trial meant it was legally impossible for me to sue pretty much whatever happened—including being gang-raped by the security staff, which is allegedly covered by the clause whereby I consent to "all necessary invasive procedures." Matthews, now more Johnny Cochran than Dr. Kildare, then reassured me that tests were already underway to ascertain definitively if the two unfortunate trialists' conditions were, in fact, down to this new drug. When I asked Matthews what exactly was the side effect the surviving one had contracted—"migraines, nausea, dizziness, insomnia, amnesia, aphasia, blindness, paralysis, which?" Dr. Matthews just nodded.

"All of them? In that case I think I'd rather have the death-hastening," I suggested.

"I'm not allowed to say. It's confidential," said Dr. Matthews.

Then by way of a clue—apparently giving a straight answer contravenes the Hippocratic Oath, but Charades doesn't—he touched his nose, snorted, and left.

"What, the patients become addicted to cocaine? I don't care. I can live with that; it might even help me with my modelling career. Hey, I could even sell a few records. Or, did that snort mean he has been transmogrified, like Odysseus's crewmen, into a pig? Shield Pharmaceuticals are actually a front of Circe of Aeaea! Well, stranger things have happened—Watergate, Rasputin surviving all those assassination attempts, Burnley beating Manchester United, and Noel Edmonds' TV comeback—Noel Edmonds being on TV in the first place."

Good old Adam calmed me down and we waited for the results of the pathology tests on my unfortunate late teammate, plus a full examination of the half-man/half-pig. We passed the time, as men like to do on long car journeys. We made lists. They ranged from the compulsory *Best Footballers Since the War*, which I separated into decades: '50s, Puskas and Di Stefano; '60s, Best and Pele; '70s, Cruyff and Beckenbauer; '80s, Platini and Maradona; '90s, Zidane and Gascoigne; and '00s, Ronaldinho and Messi (Adam twittered on about unsung goalkeepers and argued in favor of Banks and Yashin, but I overruled him.), followed by *Top Sitcom Totty*. This was won by Sally Geeson from *Bless This House*. Adam argued in favor of Portia de Rossi from *Arrested Development*, which is very sad not because she is not a beautiful woman, she is, but because that sitcom only aired a couple of year ago, and while listing Sally or Paula Wilcox from the seventies is quaint, to nominate someone you were first introduced to in your fifties is downright pervy.

As the clock ticked on, or should I say the pixels on the digital display emitted gamma rays, we tore through *Best Sandwich Possible* and *Most Difficult Sentence for a Chinese Person to Say* (it featured the adjectives "truculent," "reliable," and the name of Spanish Civil War heroine "Dolores Ibarruri"), and ended up with *Ten Things to Do Before You Die*. Adam baulked at this one for my sake, but I insisted. After he could list only one thing for himself "appear on the stage" (I disqualified his "reduce golf handicap to single figures" and "develop a six pack" as crass and stupid), I came up with my ten:

1) Finish reading James Joyce's *Ulysses*
2) Start reading James Joyce's *Ulysses*
3) Build a time machine and relive my schooldays with the knowledge I have now.

4) Organize a sleepover for Monica Bellucci, Naomi Watts, Kate Beckinsale, Zhang Ziyi, Milla Jovovich, and Kelly Holmes (with nothing on but her gold medals and running shoes).
5) Use my time machine (see 3) to repeat experience (4) ad infinitum.
6) Win the Araucaria Bank Holiday Prize Crossword.
7) Persuade Toby to stop working for "The Man."
8) Stop working for "The Man" myself. (By which I don't mean you, Alistair, you are barely a man, let alone "The Man." By "The Man," I mean a person or group asserting authority or power over another, especially in a manner experienced as being oppressive, demeaning, or threatening, such as an employer (but not you, Alistair, you wimp), the police, or a dominating racial group.
9) Score winning goal for Queen's Park Rangers against Chelsea in FA Cup Final.
10) Use time machine (see 3) to add Sally Geeson to sleepover party.

Adam asked me why I did not add watch my grandson grow up or have my last play produced to which I replied, "My grandson *may not want* me to watch him grow up. After all, my son has ended up as the direct opposite of his paternal role model, suggesting I should refrain this time from exercising grandparental influence. (Although I think his mother had a hand in steering Toby off my path of righteous poverty, and who can blame the woman?)" Adam countered that Kelly Holmes *may not want* to attend my sleepover in her medals and shoes…but *I* know she would not regret it! As for my play, well, as I said before, what is the likelihood of it becoming a fitting testament that will make me feel all cozy and fulfilled when they finally get around to pushing me out to sea in a flaming row boat? The chances are it will be mangled by one of today's impresarios who would probably rework it as a star vehicle for Shane Richie and to showcase the back catalogue of Haircut One Hundred.

As it happens, testaments are still moot since the test results came back showing no evidence of a link, whether positive or negative, between the unlicensed drug and the timing of my colleague's death. As for those *side effects*…I found out they were merely nasal congestion (very sophisticated gesturing code, Dr. Matthews; why the great Alan Turing would have been stretched to cracking that one!) and caused not by our experimental drug regime, but by a viral infection, aka a cold.

FC Naylor

P.S. I confess that most of *my* "ten tasks" are even more challenging than the Labors of Hercules (despite being two fewer) and have lobbied Adam to concentrate on realizing *his* not unreasonable target of appearing on stage. So I have rung his wife, telling her not to stand in the way of his lifetime ambition to perform.

16. Saturday, June 18

Yet another week spent mopping up the detritus of the week before. I seem to be trapped in a cycle of retaliation that would make Israeli vs. Palestine, Alien vs. Predator, and Roy Keane vs. Everyone Who Is Not Roy Keane look like South Africa's Truth and Reconciliation Committee. This time the grudgeholder is not a movement, but someone I know. Mrs. Gold has accused me of libel and threatened legal proceedings against the newspaper— go ahead, I think media moguls should be more accountable, too. (*Editor's Note: This is also neither the view of The Commentator, nor of any individual or body within, allied to, or subsidiary to Parnell Media Holdings or the Parnell Group PLC.*) The basis of her suit is that she has never once held back husband, Adam, from pursuing his dream on the amateur stage. In fact, she would love to see him out more evenings so she can watch repeats of *The Sopranos* and documentaries on BBC4 instead of *Britain's Got Talent* and *World Wrestling Entertainment Diva Search*. He is using her as an excuse because, quite simply, Adam is "s**t scared that he will be s**t." Now, I applaud Esther for being the only person ballsy enough to threaten to use the courts against a feeble dying man like myself, but I was very disappointed to learn about her passionate conviction not through a visit, or a phone call, or even a letter…but via Facebook!

I'm no Luddite, though I still retain affection for Captain Swing, and I don't mean Frank Sinatra. In fact, I am writing on a word processor as I…er, write, and I allowed Pavla to set up a Facebook account of me "for your fans, Mr. Naylor." Adam describes Pavla as "Cordelia to my Lear"…not sure who gets the better deal. But why is it that the more varied means of communication we have and the more accessible to others we become, the less we smell the skin, see the face, or even hear the voice of those who wish to approach us?

There are now more mobile masts per square mile than there are erections on Old Compton Street. There are cell phones, cordless phones, landlines, Skype, and sockets to plug in your equipment in cafes, on trains and planes, and whole WiFi towns (well, Swindon), but nobody actually uses those opportunities to talk. Instead, they use Windows Live Messenger and the emails through the TV screen, your 3G, Blackberry, the iPhone, or worse than that…text messages. Alexander Bell, Thomas Edison, Antonio Meucci, and Elisha Gray pioneered the transmission of the human voice across great distances to bring us closer together, to reduce our dependence on writing, and free the illiterate from their prison of silence. Everything since then has been designed to keep us apart, so we never have to actually be in each other's presence or even in earshot. Emails, texts, and message boards are the communication equivalents of the drive-by shooting—strike with a written message and then run away. Texting is for cowards. It's one stage up from scratching slander onto toilet walls. If you've got something to say, say it to my face not my Facebook, or at least direct it to my ears so I can respond.

Now, a well-crafted letter, that is another thing entirely, and I received an example of this only yesterday. Letters are not short-hand by remote control, sidebars, or crawlers spat out by people whose attention is elsewhere. Letters are expressions of feelings and ideas personal to the author, tailored precisely for the needs of the reader, constructed with logic and grace, and demanding a decent investment of time and emotion. Those letters requiring the most application and labor, I admit, tend to be those written by kidnappers who not only have to cut out each individual letter from a different newspaper or magazine, but also have to be careful not to leave fingerprints. Now I am not promoting abductions for ransom as a lifestyle choice, but when you get a letter from someone who does, at least then you know that they really were thinking of you and no one else when they wrote it. All these vowel-less texts and grammar-free emails are designed to be written in the least amount of time possible. Why? Because the author basically wants to be able to stop communicating with you as soon as possible since they have better things to do. Hence, all the abbreviations…even "email" is an abbreviation for "electronic mail," and "text" is, OMG, technically the text version of your mobile telephone's "short message service."

Thankfully, the aforementioned letter did not come from the Scorpio Serial Killer, Southwark Parking Services, or the Ciudad Juarez Cartel, but from my daughter-in-common-law, Mary. At first, I was shocked to read in Mary's first sentence that she, frail female and pregnant, had received a kicking! Then I realized that was just a headline to draw me into the body of her missive and, when the facts were fully revealed, it tuned out the perpetrator of this savage podal assault was not some ASBO crackhead, but the baby moving inside her. Quite why she chose to use the front cover of the *Daily Sport* ("Diana found alive s***ing off David Beckham…fake photos scandal!") as a template to hook me in to her epistle, I am not sure. At least I was relieved not to find advertising for Latex Lovers' Chat Lines or Linsey Dawn Mckenzie's latest group sex DVD in the corner of the page, and I forgave the letter's stylistic quirk for its content, which turned out to be very generous toward me:

> "Dear FC,
>
> I know you did not see much of Toby when he was growing up, but he tells me that he learned a lot from you anyway, such as always being honest and true to yourself. When I was at high school and even later at college—and I see it with my mom's friends, too—everybody is so bothered about what other people think of them…."

Mary then gives examples of her friends who all seem to have surnames as first names like Taylor, Madison, and Brooke, or are named after deli food like Brie and Chanterelle. Then she returns to her subject…me.

"But, you are different. You don't care if you are an asshole. I mean, if other people think you are an asshole, and that's what I want for my child when he is born."

Mary then explains that she doesn't want her and Toby's child actually to be an asshole like its grandfather, but to have principles and be prepared to stick to them. I found this both flattering and admirable, although I fear that pressure to be so virtuous can sometimes misfire. I sometimes wonder if Toby would have been less superficial, materialistic, and mercenary if I hadn't told him that when he grew up it was his personal duty to save the world after my generation had so f***ed it up—too onerous an expectation of one's offspring perhaps.

Mary signs off by hoping that I get a chance to meet my grandchild. "Signs off" because it was a letter with an actual signature at the end instead of an algebraic qualifier followed by a smiley face! A letter that examines the past in order to see more clearly the future, rather than being obsessed with relentlessly extending the present.

This intuitive advocacy for the written word spurred me to take another gander at my final play, *Lamplight,* my interest in which had been resurrected during our previous debate on legacy, a concept, ever since the 2012 Olympic bid, currently attached in the public imagination exclusively to running tracks, car parks, and additional bus routes. As it happens, my temptation to succumb to the sin of vanity was thankfully erased when I found that the manuscript has gone missing and, seeing as I only had the one paper copy, the debate on producing it can finally be put to rest.

LOL **FC Naylor**

P. S. *Facebook* isn't so bad after all. I have received a posting from Sally Geeson saying she is up for coming round for tea. (Still no word from Kelly Holmes or the others as yet.)

17. Saturday, June 25

Had to tell off Pavla this week because of the noise upstairs. My evenings used to be relatively quiet while her pan-European flat-mates were out working extra shifts in poultry processing plants, waiting tables, or sleeping before a predawn trip to a fruit farm. Now, when they all get back, they seem to have gotten into the habit of moving the furniture and raising their voices. In my head, I imagine some sort of Slavic orgy, Stakhanovite in its intensity, Hapsburg in its decadence. Pavla assures me it is nothing of the sort, but the image remains, and will remain as long as I want it to. Never let them control your thoughts. (I've had my head stuck in enough Computational Axial Tomography and Functional Magnetic Resonance Imaging scanners to know that.) But this new girl, Mira from Montenegro, definitely lights up something in my brain. Allegedly the Warsaw Pact Four are arguing over how to optimize the distribution of territory in the flat between the four of them. All it needs is Matthius from Prague to get thrown out of the window and we have the start of a new Thirty Years War.

Pavla made it up to me by taking me to shop for baby clothes in Mothercare in Peckham. I thought that so-called *musician* who's been hanging around her would turn out to be bad news. For a start, he is as much a musician as I am one of *The Archers*. Listening to the stuff is not enough to make you one of them, and owning a bass guitar bought from Argos does not make you

Charles Mingus anymore than possessing a Fisher Space Pen makes me an astronaut. Therefore, I told her that now that Poland was in the EU she didn't need to glue herself to a British citizen in order to stay here, still less did she need a kid to raise her self-esteem and, if necessary, I could ask Adam to sort out any "trouble" she had got into with this philandering troubadour. Well, I am afraid that Pavla took issue with me. For a start, she is a Catholic and opposed to all abortions, to which I countered, "Come on, you have already committed the mortal sin of sex before marriage. In for a penny, in…" She then assured me that she had not slept with "Cosmo" (what sort of name is that for a man raised in Orpington?) before adding that Adam would be the last doctor she would ever let near her. I had to agree on the last one.

Since I put my foot in it about the acting, Esther Gold has her husband sleeping alone on the sofa. Frustrated, Adam is more likely to get Pavla *in* the club than out of it. Anyhow, it turns out the 0-6 months Mothercare clothes are not for any notional future Pavlette, but for Toby junior. I said it was way too early to be buying presents; the kid wasn't due 'til December. Pavla tried bravely to conceal it, but her look explained why it was probably better to get something right now—even though we had to buy everything in green (I did not trust that tiny sonogram and I have heard of babies changing sex in the womb.), since the gender-neutral orange reminded me too much of Guantanamo Bay, which ruled out the entire *Tigger* clothing line.

Not sure I like the whole One Hundred Acre Wood *milieu* anyway. What sort of a role model is Winnie the Pooh? Distinguished jointly by his greed and his stupidity, he makes Joey from *Friends* look like Immanuel Kant, and his friend Eeyore's disabling melancholy is enough to douse the brio of Ruby Wax (if only he would).

I looked at the other branded items in the shop—slippers shaped like steam engines harking back to the days of the Industrial Revolution when women could not vote, workers could not join unions, Catholics could not stand for office, and those charming engines pulled trains full of cotton spun by white employees paid very little, having been picked by black slaves paid nothing at all. However, if you walk past the Thomas the Tank Engine footwear dedicated to one of the most polluting industries of them all, you only end up buying nightwear that is a tribute to the effects of much more modern sources of energy. Pajamas featuring the Hulk, schizoid mutant victim of nuclear weapons testing with anger management issues, or Spiderman, traumatized loner poisoned by radioactive toxins, who turns vigilante to assuage guilt over the manslaughter of his uncle. With this in mind, I jotted down what I consider more appropriate role models for children—historical characters, not imaginary ones.

What could be a more propitious time to import some real life role models for the young than today when the only live action celebrities that kids know after they outgrow these cartoon fantasies are people like Paris Hilton, Lindsay Lohan, Amy Winehouse, and Pete Doherty whose principal expertise seems to be in racking up drunk driving convictions and not eating. At least when I was young, when we got drunk or high, we were able to stay on the road (*pace* Marc Bolan, but his hair probably got in the way of his eyes), and the King of Rock and Roll himself would rather die than skip a meal (and did). Celebrity in proportion to achievement, fame the reward for rare talent or hard work, respect earned by sacrifice…those are the lessons I want to teach Toby junior. Therefore, let's have the images of some real heroes deserving of their status emblazoning pencil cases, mouse pads, lunch boxes, and transfer tattoos.

In chronological order I recommend:

1) **Prometheus** - He took on the Gods to emancipate the human race with his gift of fire and suffered for it (48 percent of 16-24 year olds polled recently thought Prometheus was a make of a condom, the other 52 percent, a gym shoe).

2) **Morgan Le Fey** - She took on patriarchy—both the temporal (King Arthur) and spiritual (Merlin) *and l*ooked like Helen Mirren.

3) **Gerrard Winstanley** – He took on Cromwell's military dictatorship and tried to replace the monarchy with democracy.

4) **George Loveless** - The Tolpuddle Martyr who "raise(d) the watchword liberty," but is included neither in the 26,000-entry Cambridge Biographical Enyclopedia nor Wikipedia, although Limahl off *Kajagoogoo* is! Get his likeness on your dressing gown!

5) **Toussaint L'Ouverture** - Freed himself and his fellow African slaves in Haiti years before Wilberforce. Eventually became a violent autocratic, but you can't have everything.

7) **Tecumseh** - The Che Guevara of North America, a Shawnee Indian who united a continent against its European invaders, dying heroically in the process.

8) **Alexandra Kollontai -** Russian revolutionary socialist and feminist, advocating sexual liberation and gender equality half a century before Friedan, Steinem, Millet, and Greer and opposed the Communist Party's creep toward corruption. She was also the world's first woman ambassador. Only Buffy the Vampire Slayer compares.

9) **Dolores Ibarruri -** *La Pasionaria* fought Franco, founded Eurocommunism, and invented the slogan, "*No passaran!*" plus her only son died defeating the Third Reich at Stalingrad. Swap your Bratz and Barbie backpacks for one of hers or one of…

10) **Mildred "Babe Zaharias" Didrikson -** The 5'5" Olympic athletics star winning gold in the hurdles and javelin, silver in the high jump; U.S. National Basketball Champion; winner of the grand slam of golf majors including the U.S. Open one month after cancer surgery—the greatest sportsperson who ever lived alongside…

11) **Muhammad Ali -** "The Greatest"…boxer, poet, preacher, and protester…they knocked him down, he got back up.

12) **Augusto Boal -** The Brazilian whose book *Teatro do Oprimido* turned me into a playwright and opened the minds of millions of rural poor in Latin America.

13) **Brian Clough -** Son of a factory worker, 251 goals in 273 matches, he was youngest manager in the League. Made Derby County champions in 1972, got Forest promoted in 1977, League Champions in 1978, European Champions in 1979 and again in 1980. Discovered Martin O'Neill and

Roy Keane. Twatted a yob for invading the pitch. Stood on the picket line with the miners and fought racism with the ANL.

14) **Dorothy Stang** - American Nun who defied the Church to live in the Amazon jungle to defend the poor. Shot dead by a landowner's hitman.

15) **Malalai Joya** - Female Afghan democrat who took on the warlords, drug dealers, and Fundamentalists armed only with the truth and a bigger pair of *cojones* than the entire AK-47, RPG-toting Mujahideen put together.

16) **Spock** - The science officer not the pediatric doctor. Vulcan brain joins human heart. Took a bullet (well, radioactive meltdown actually) to save the Enterprise, his friends, and the entire Galaxy in *Star Trek II Wrath of Khan*.

In the end, I bought a car seat for my grandchild-to-be, non-gender specific with *Britax* written on it, some boy band, I think.

FC Naylor

18. Saturday, July 2

The usual small-minded pedants wrote in to complain about the historical accuracy of my list, claiming that neither Prometheus nor Morgan Le Fey were real people. I wrote back, telling them Jesus doesn't exist either, but that doesn't stop him from being a role model. Interestingly, no one questioned Spock being on the list, but then he has been on TV a lot, which for many people is as real as you can get. In addition, Britax rang offering me money to endorse their car seats in a TV ad. They even suggested paying my repeat fees to my future grandchild. I said I thought his grandmother could probably make sure he is financially secure.

Threw all the complaining letters in the bin, only for Pavla to rebuke me for: 1) not recycling, and 2) not shredding them. I should shred all my correspondence, she says, in case someone tries to steal my identity! I said I am an ageing, underemployed bachelor dying in a bedsit near the Elephant and Castle; anybody who wants to be me, can. She told me I was exaggerating, not about the dying bit, mind you, about the bedsit—it is actually three rooms. However, I took her up on the recycling thing. Red and Green have never clashed in my vision. It is the capitalist imperative of constant growth that drives the unsustainable consumption that causes deforestation, traffic, air pollution, erosion of habitats, over-fishing, global warming, and so on. So, a brake on growth will prevent developing countries from enjoying the lifestyle we First Worlders take for granted? As far as I can see, the rise in GDP in Brazil is spent by the middle class on facelifts and building walls around their villas, while the poor use the extra cash to buy cocaine and automatic weapons. But then, I suppose that *is* the lifestyle Los Angeles takes for granted.

So, I went on an environmental march organized by the Green Party to protest the building of a new incinerator in the borough and volunteered to get on the platform at the rally in Burgess Park to suggest some solutions. The Campaign Group MP on before me concentrated on taxing aviation fuel, which alienated a lot of the assembled who mumble about the rising cost of their next ski holiday, so I decided to go more *big picture* while focusing on the twin *A*s and attacked advertising and architects.

I told the assembled cyclists and celiacs, vegans, virgins, freshers, and farmer's marketers how I came across *Eyes Wide Shut* on Film Four. (Yes, I am obsessed with this film, mainly because the last thing I had published before this column was my letter to *Sight and Sound* comparing it to Jean Rollin's 1970 sex-horror hybrid *La Vampire Nue,* but without the laughs. It is that bad. The worst film I've seen by a good director since Adam brought around Ang Lee's *The Hulk*, which is even worse than Paul Verhoeven's *Showgirls.)* If I had been wearing purple pajamas, I would have burst out of them and turned green with rage just watching it. Adam claimed it wasn't the DVD he had intended us to watch and that one of his children must have swapped it with the Lars Von Trier movie by accident. Why on earth a ten year old would want to watch Bjork and Catherine Deneuve in *Dancer in the Dark,* a film about capital punishment, rather than a super hero movie, God only knows. Therefore, I playfully accused Adam of secretly fancying Eric Bana, but he got rather cross and insisted it certainly was the Bjork movie that he had intended to bring around. I said *Dancer in the Dark* was a musical, so he was still gay. Anyway *Eyes Wide Shut* is truly shit; you must never watch it, but that is neither here nor there.

Anyway, before that over-art-directed w**k movie, with a score so atonal it makes John Cage sound like Kylie Minogue, consumed three precious hours of my rapidly evaporating life, there screened a very effective advert by Ikea demonstrating how "home is the most important place in the world," by which we have to conclude that people should stay indoors more often, ideally, never leaving their homes. (Not very good copy for a retail outlet that refused to do mailorder.) In fact, the advert implies one should preserve Sunday as home-with-the-family day, given it is one of the few days you are not out at work, and you'll not be leaving your home ("the most important place in the world") to trawl around Ikea like some poor fisherman looking for the last sturgeon in the Black Sea.... I will personally pay for ads in the cinema and on TV launching a "life is as good as can be expected, you don't need anything else, buy nothing" campaign. That is my Green message.

Landfills poisoning the earth and using up space. Incinerators polluting air and using up energy. Recycling plants, billions spent researching how to blast rubbish into orbit or trap it underground, the galactic equivalent of chucking it out the window or sweeping it under the carpet. Don't recycle more, how about using less? If this government says no to taxing your dustbins, but says yes to building more houses, then at least build them without cellars and without attics. People buy more than they need only because they have cellars and attics in which to store the excess stuff. Ban storage space and see how houses without attics, being shorter, improve our skylines. It would save money on lagging, too. And, the absence of a *cellar* would cut down on crime. Bomb-making materials, corpses, stolen goods...are all kept in cellars. Without them, terrorism, murder, and theft drops. Ban garages and lock-ups, and the rate of abductions and sex crimes would also decline. Even better, ban cupboards, then people will only be able to buy what they can fit on the floor. Roof racks, trailers, garden sheds—they should all go, too. It's like the physics of the expansion of gases, for as long as there is space to put things we will buy things to fill those spaces. Pockets, lets get rid of them; make everyone wear tight-fitting body suits like Olympic swimmers or on Star Trek.... Captain Kirk never once used a pocket and he conquered the universe and had loads of sex doing it.

The environmentalist audience seemed puzzled by the Socratic route I took to conclude that the advertising of consumer goods and the architecture of homes should be in our cross hairs, but they all rose as one when I finished off with a Pablo Neruda quote in Spanish. The fact that it was from *Ode to the Tomato* rather than one of his poems railing against Chilean fascism did not appear to tarnish its glow. I only hope the tomato in question was organic.

Later Adam came round with a DVD of *Guys and Dolls* or *Gays and Dolls*, as I like to call it. He is auditioning for the part of "Society Max" in the *Finchley Mummers* amateur production. It isn't the musical I would have written (Brecht and Weill already wrote that), but it was most enjoyable, though. Jean Simmons has got that posh and nice, but-could-be-really-naughty quality that Cressida used to have (and she delivered on the promise, Alistair). Unfortunately, some of the quieter sequences were interrupted by the sound of more furniture scraping upstairs.

FC Naylor

19. Saturday, July 9

Thank you for the correspondence regarding my use of the word "gay" in last week's column. Some of you felt I was using the word disparagingly. Well, I wasn't, but should I choose to, I will. The pejorative connotation attributed by some readers is misplaced, but even were it to have been correctly identified, that would not be a criticism as such. You would also have to follow through and demonstrate that gayness in the context in which it is used does entail the negative qualities proposed by the user of the word. And if you cannot follow that line of logic, then you must be retarded…sorry, have "special educational needs." Which by the way is not, per se, a denigrating comment either since the top 10 percent of school children defined as "gifted and talented" are also officially designated as having special educational needs. Do your homework before taking on a man who is so friendless and physically lazy that semantics are his daily exercise. By the way, "denigrate" means to "blacken" and is not a word I normally use because I, and my Negro friends, consider it racist; or, should I say my "colored" friends? If not, then why is the most pioneering and venerated race rights organization in the USA still called the National Association for the Advancement of Colored People (NAACP)? And don't think this only applies to Americans—or as I prefer to say, people of America. (Incidentally, congratulations on the anniversary of your Independence last week. I look forward to joining in the celebrations when the independence, in which you take pride, is finally conceded to the Northern Marianas Islands, the Marshall Islands, the Federated States of Micronesia, Palau, Guam, and Puerto Rico, too.)

On the subject of prejudice, I have felt a little under the weather this week—probably why I failed to attend the Ambassador at St. James's fireworks party on the 4th—and visited Dr. Matthews. Adam could not attend with me because it was the day of his audition and he had scheduled an entire day of dance practice and vocal exercises, which was very gay of him. I would say "homosexual," except that I haven't heard that word since it was whispered in some black and white (Caucasian) movie about blackmailing public figures in the early sixties. (I must confess I haven't listened to any of the recent debates in the General Synod of the Anglican Communion, but I understand the word has been coming up quite a lot there.)

Dr. Matthews had a nurse check my vitals, but nothing measurable showed up, although there was a consensus that I probably had deteriorated, based on the observation that I was looking old. But do they mean David Attenborough-old or Joan Collins-old, who both still look sharp and like they are getting fun out of life? Or, do they mean *Last of the Summer Wine*-old? The silence my enquiry met with, spoke volumes. Now, I never was a ruddy youth, nor equipped with an athletic frame, so a few more wrinkles, a greyer complexion, more exposed scalp, and an unsteady walk are not, for me, the terrifying prospects they might be for a model, a sportsman, or that Frenchman who walked on a wire between the Twin Towers. What does concern me, though, is the reaction that "looking old" gets. Don't get me wrong, I look forward to having people offer me their seat on the grounds that I am infirm and stop mugging me on the grounds that I won't have anything worth nicking (iPod, Blackberry, cash); I don't even mind being spoken to unnecessarily loudly and slowly.

What I do not want is people assuming, as they do when they meet someone old, that they only know of old people-things like bath chairs, lunch clubs, bowls, Vera Lynn, Viagra—that they are forever stuck in the past. I am not looking forward to being treated like that, especially since I am not that old—I am not a grandfather yet, I am only Sixty, I could marry Catherine Zeta

Jones or Billie Piper *and* satisfy them—I am not going to reach old age either. I just look old. So, I decided to play up to it—if they expect old, I will give them old.

So, when I left Harley Street with a specimen cylinder and some iron tablets as my reward (I prefer lollipops personally.) and stumbled toward Baker Street tube, I was delighted to be asked directions for Madam Tussaud's (which any idiot can see is that huge building with the massive queue outside, 200 yards down the road).

"The waxworks, eh?" I replied in my best Dick Emery *Charles Maynard Kithchener Lampwick* voice.

"Walk up the street and then turn left where the cinema used to be. Tsk. That's a Blockbuster Video now. Keep going till you reach the old Palace of Variety. That's gone, too; one of them Internet cafes today. Cross the green where they used to have the old bare-knuckled fights; that's a Holmes Place Health and Fitness Centre now, you know, all that poncy Pilates and Capoiera stuff now… and you're opposite the adventure playground. That was an air raid shelter in the war. Those were the days, eh? People were friendlier then…well, apart from the Germans. Oh, you are German. Pass the amusement arcade. That was a Magic Lantern show…cost a farthing. Anyway, you'll see this big housing estate. I remember when that was all fields, you know—before the Industrial Revolution—happy days. There's a mini roundabout. We used to burn heretics there, just after the Reformation. We didn't have TV then, had to make your own entertainment…. You'll see a pub. That used to be a burial mound. Course, that was in the Bronze Age. You'll reach the gravel path. That used to be igneous rock, but then tectonic shifts in the Ice Age put a stop to that. You'll see a football club. I remember when that used to be dense primeval forest. A big herd of brachiosauri used to graze there. Next-door is Madame Tussaud's. 'Course that used to be a swirling ball of super-heated nitrogen, hydrogen, and methane gasses, but that was over ten billion years ago…before your time."

The tourist probably went on to tell his friends about the weird things this "old man" said to him today (I freely admit I look older than my years). Not a male person, a tall person, a white person, or an English person… an *old* person, because that is what you see first. But oldness isn't like gender, race, build, or nationality. You aren't *born* that way. Old people weren't always old. They haven't witnessed the world through old eyes the whole of their lives. Old is what they are now. The vast majority of their lives they were not old at all (excluding those Japanese centenarians who remember the Mammoth). They've been a child hungry for an ice cream, a teenager obsessed with sex, an adult at peak physical strength, a parent getting used to their first baby, and middle-aged worrying where they've gone wrong. They've held our attitudes and they've shared our perspectives. They've even held our prejudice against old people. They've already had our present and our past. The only real difference between them and us is that they've seen our future, too.

And, speaking of the future, Adam is going to fulfill his lifetime ambition to perform on stage! Opening night is scheduled for late autumn; he is seventh down the cast list in (the catamite classic) *Guys and Dolls*!

FC Naylor

P.S. Pavla dropped a bombshell just before we went to press. She delivered to me a handwritten invitation to a rehcarsed reading of a new play, which she is in. Everybody seems to be getting all-theatrical, apart from me! Apparently, the noise upstairs has been her and her friends rehearsing—though, why they should feel the need to shift furniture around for a simple reading, I don't get. The name of the author of the play is missing from the flyer, but I used Google Translator to furnish me with the English version of the title. In Polish it is *Swiatla z Lampa*. It translates into English as *Lamplight*.

The reason Pavla did not put the author's name on the invitation is because it was written by me.

20. Saturday, July 16

I used to have nightmares about being thrown a surprise birthday party. The awkward rearranging of emotions that follows having reconciled oneself to a solitary night in, in front of *Match of the Day* or a foreign film on Channel 4, that informal *dejeuner-a-deux*, or some other smokescreen your partner/family member/work colleague has concocted in order to blind you to the impending truth.

Luckily, I have had no partner for a while, no siblings, and my parents are long dead—and how often does one get the chance to relish being an orphan, bachelor and only child? Therefore, the probabilities of facing 1) an ego-choking paucity of celebrants that make the mourners at Fred West's funeral look like the Hajj, 2) a drunk ex-lover with a score to settle, 3) family members you have had no contact with for years…because you have goddamn *reasons* for having no contact for years, or 4) having to make a speech…have all thankfully always been remote. To have a surprise premier of your unedited, untried, and out-of-date final play staged in your neighbor's flat by a bunch of twenty-something, East European migrants whose command of English makes the Scouser from *Girls Aloud* sound like Dorothy Parker, is to endure a living hell. Or, so I anticipated….

There were color invitations to this local premier on account of Jerzy who moonlights at Kopy Town. All that distinguished this invite from the genuine article was a lack of map and directions, but then the show was being performed upstairs. I tried to talk Pavla out of it, but she said her favourite Pope, John Paul II (aka Karol Wojtyla), had been a playwright in her native Poland before he took up Holy Orders, so she knew plays must be important. I pointed out JPII was also a goalkeeper, that didn't mean we had to play five-a-side in her flat. She also said that she had sent out invitations, so it was too late to cancel. I wondered who on earth she had invited, seeing as I didn't see anyone apart from Adam and rarely, Cressida. The answer came back—Adam and Cressida. (Actually, she had also invited Toby, but he was now back in the U.S.)

The set was fantastically realistic. Or, would have been…had my play been set in a second floor flat, rather than the pithead of a Yorkshire mine. And, it wasn't as bad as I remembered. The cast had to double up as wives, strikers, police, scabs, and politicians, and were universally terrible, but the dialogue—what I could discern from a Babel of accents that made Dino de Laurentiis's 1970s' international action movies with Sophia Loren, Max Von Sidow, Richard Harris, Omar Sharif, Romy Schneider, Robert Vaughn, etc., sound like the RSC—seemed okay. The audience seemed to actually care whether the bloke occupying the pit all on his own came out alive or not. I told Paula that, coincidentally, as a result of Thatcher shutting down the pits in 1985, we ended up importing most of our coal from Poland! She started crying at this point…probably felt guilty. Adam said the play was like *Billy Elliot*—but without Billy Elliot! I said that was as stupid as calling a movie "like *Jaws*, but without the shark." Or, *X-Men,* without any X-Men. Adam's got bloody musicals on the brain, and now he has seen *Lamplight,* it means I've got to go and see him in *Guys and Dolls* and I never liked the Runyon stories in the first place—a poor man's O. Henry meets an even poorer Dashiell Hammett. Hopefully, I'll croak before then.

Cressida—this venerable publication's major shareholder and of whom your esteemed editor would in modern vernacular be described as *her bitch*—said it was "…full of passion, commitment, and politics aside a universal and timeless tale about sacrifice, heroism, and the preservation of ideals." To which I replied, "Shame our son wasn't able to sacrifice some time to see it." Well,

I got a ticking off for saying that. I know this column cannot be described as a vehicle for confession and personal redemption, but I will take the opportunity to print a little apology. (And not for calling Alistair Sinclair, Cressida Parnell's bitch. That I will never take back.) According to Cressida, the reason that Toby's life choices bear all the hallmarks of a sustained campaign to annul all his father's ideals is not, contrary to my embittered accusations, because his mother turned him against me on account of being a rubbish husband. In fact, Cressida assures me *she* always promoted my values of equality of respect and active social conscience (I think she draws the line at wealth redistribution, the common ownership of the means of production, and the levelling of all churches and private schools in order to grow crops). Rather, it was Toby's own shrewd awareness that he could never live up to such lofty expectations that was the catalyst for his playboy wanderlust. In conclusion, Cressida never poisoned his ear and, if I had not pressured him so much politically to succeed where I had failed, he might well have become an expert on fascism with intimate knowledge of the Paris Commune, as opposed to an expert on fashion with intimate knowledge (literarily) of Paris Hilton.

So, a mixed evening, then. The play was better than I remembered, but I pissed off Adam and upset Pavla. My ex liked the show, but it's my fault my son missed it.

FC Naylor

Note to Readers: The Commentator newspaper, its Board of Directors, shareholders, and editorial staff would all like to dissociate themselves from the opinion expressed herein regarding the characterization of the relationship between Cressida Parnell and Alistair Sinclair.

But we in the print shop all agree he is her bitch!

21. Saturday, July 23

No column was published this week.

22. Saturday, July 30

Sorry for last week's non-appearance. Contrary to rumors, I was not banned from writing it because of my views about the editor (who is forced to sleep chained to the leg of my ex-wife's bed wearing a leather gimp mask), nor have the printers been banned from printing it due to their unauthorized addition to the previous column. Alistair did get very steamed up about that and in his inevitable obloquy managed to reference the Pulitzer Prize, the First Amendment to the U.S. Constitution, the legacy of *Relation aller Fürnemmen und gedenckwürdigen Historien,* which is the world's first newspaper, Woodward and Bernstein, Arthur Scargill, and Joseph Goebbels all in his opening sentence. He did have a word with the printers, too, but the Father of the Chapel still remembers me on the picket line at Wapping supporting SOGAT and the NGA in 1986.

No, the real reason it never got published, was it never got written. The reason it never got written, was I got drunk.

I don't normally get drunk, but it was not a normal week. First, Toby's wife rang from the States to reiterate that my son did not blame me for anything. Then Toby rang to apologize for not having had the courage to tell me in person before. I countered that telling me by telephone from ten thousand miles away is still not strictly in person. Well, I had to say something to stop the conversation from turning into the final reel of the afternoon movie on Hallmark Television. Although that equivalence had already been undermined when he started explaining that contrary to my published allegation, he did not have full intimate knowledge of Paris Hilton and volunteered the biological details why...

This, on top of the play, meant things were getting a little overheated and not surprisingly I had a migraine. Pavla heard me moaning through the wall and called Adam—so there was more *Waltons*-style apologizing (the TV family based on the book *Spencer's Mountain,* not the Union-busting retail plutocrats of the same name). The apologizing was one-way, mind you, and not from me. I was distracted by something. What was it? Oh, yes, the hydrogen bombs going off in my head. Imagine Sir Alex Ferguson's older, angrier brother, just after you have conceded the last minute goal that gives Manchester City the Champions League crown, trying to be heard (successfully) over two 12-cylinder Rolls-Royce Merlin engines strapped to each ear. The immediate sacrifice of the lives of every man, woman, and child I have ever liked (not that many, to be sure), plus my complete collection of QPR programmes 1958-1967 is what I offered God just to temporarily abate the pain. Attempted filicide? Abraham of Ur has nothing on what I was prepared to do to please the big guy.

Well, Adam drives me all the way to the Ansdell Goodrich Laboratories so Dr. Matthews can see me personally. Meanwhile, I am begging to be taken to an abbatoir or a morphine-wholesaler, whichever is nearer. The codeine Adam had given me is not working. The sound of his mobile phone ringing, which he won't answer because he is driving, is enough to drown the bells of Notre Dame on a Sunday and straighten Quasimodo's back, and by the time we reach the gates of the compound, I am not afraid that I might be dying, I am wishing it. A wish, which might come true given that Pavla is praying in Latin with the speed and power of Jarmila Kratochvilova in her 1984 steroid prime.

The porters wheel me in to the consulting room where Dr. Matthews' Parsee secretary, Leila, greets us with the news that...Dr. Matthews is not there. Adam looks as if he might be about to complain—a first in my experience; I would die happy having witnessed that, but doesn't get around to it because it turns out the calls to his mobile, all of which he ignored, were from Leila…telling him that Dr. Matthews is not there. But, she adds in her most reassuring voice, he would not have been able to help me anyway since the drug trial has been cancelled by the DOH! In fact, he's currently at a meeting at the National Institute for Clinical Excellence going over the details.

Then, suddenly, all the pain drained away. Pavla, who was on the phone pleading with that graduate from the Khmer Rouge Academy of Conflict Resolution who runs the day nursery where her twin wards were attending that day, finally hangs up and there is silence…blissful, terminal silence.

Adam tries to cheer me up on the way home. Although all trials of my potential lifesaver have been suspended throughout the EU, it is still legal to test them on humans in a medical facility on the outskirts of Ashkhabad, Turkmenistan. Then, again, it is legal to store spent uranium fuel rods in your compost in Ashkhabad, Turkmenistan. Not completely assuaged, Adam shifts gear and tells me the results recorded so far in the trial pointed to the drug *not* stalling the VHD anyway. In fact, the only memorable consequence of the drug trials was the extraordinary extent to which the placebo outperformed it, the main subject of conversation on statistician blogs worldwide. The cherry on the cake was the news, when we got home, that because she was twenty minutes late collecting Pebbles and Bam Bam from "Child's Play—Primrose Hill's premier learning-centred activity programme"—for privileged little bastards—Pavla got fired.

So, the two of us disappointees both got very drunk, and that is why I couldn't write my column.

Actually, that's why I couldn't write my column on Thursday. *I was* sober by Friday, but I didn't write it then either because I didn't feel like it. Pavla, who was outside the Job Centre by 8:45 the next morning with an updated CV in one hand, while speed-dialing employment agencies with the other, blamed my truculent (not to say outspoken and aggressive) rejection of her encouragement that I work that day, on my drinking.

"Drink makes women happy and sentimental, but with men, it always makes them want to fight," she asserted. "Fighting all over the world would never happen if the alcohol did not make the men adversarial."

"In which case, it doesn't make women sentimental, it makes them stupid, if you believe that."

That sentence seemed more graceful at the time. I think perhaps I wasn't completely sober after all.

I continued. "Because how do you explain the Iraq/Iran war? Two million dead Muslims didn't have a shandy between them! What was going on there? Overdose on caffeine? Six cups of Red Mountain, time for a border incursion…. and, of course, World War II. Did not the German Nazi Party begin its climb to power after the *Beer Hall Putsch* in 1923? Yes, it did. It all started in a pub in Munich. At the start of the evening, they were just a bunch of ordinary lads having a few beers at the bar. Granted, a bit right wing to begin with, but not like UKIP or anything. However, the more you drink, the more set in your beliefs you become. "Hey, I'm really good looking. I could have Marlene Dietrich. Now."

"Marlene Dietrich? I turned her down!"

So, they drink and they drink and everything's fine until closing time—because at eleven o'clock the whole of Munich shuts down. "Wait a minute, I want to drink more!"

Then one bright spark shouts, "Time zones! The pubs are still open in Poland!" And off they go, goose-stepping, lager louts march into Poland!

"Ten pints of Old Warsaw, Innkeeper!" And, soon the town is drunk dry.

"Wait, everyone, it's Happy Hour in Belgium!"

Beer-swilling stormtroopers march across Europe, "Your finest Absinthe, *Monsieur l'hotelier.*"

Then they get out the Michelin Guide to Europe, "Look, it's Beaujolais Nouveau season in France!"

No wonder Kurt Waldheim couldn't remember what he did in the war! He was completely rat-arsed! "I was only taking orders…a schnapps for Himmler and the Fuhrer will have a Babycham".

And the rest of Germany went, "I will have a Babycham!" And where was the only place you could get Babycham in 1940? A wine bar in Hove. Cue the Battle of Britain!

This did not go down well. I don't know whether it was the mention of Poland or simply the fact I was shouting at her, but once again I upset Pavla. And, once again, she excused me. Not because of the booze, though. She said because I was ill and because I was angry about being ill.

I denied this. "I am not angry because I am ill. I am angry because the world is a shit hole and the only people with the power to make it better are the people who like it that way. That's why I used to be a writer, I said, 'to pass that message on and try to change things.' According to Cressy, it cost me my son and now I can't even do that anymore."

So my weekly column did not get written last week and I even considered packing it in. A weekly drinking binge is an inviting alternative, but then something happened to change my mind… but I will tell you about that next time.

FC Naylor

23. Saturday, August 5

I lied. Nothing happened to change my mind.

I was just worried that you would stop reading my column unless I put a cliffhanger in at the end. Internal market research showed my temporary replacement for last week—the head teacher of some academy school sponsored by KwikFit, Pfizer, or some other business "doing a Jesuit" and trying to catch their future customers at age seven—got this column a higher approval rating than me. What I want to know is: How can a newspaper do market research on which bits of it the readers like most? Doesn't it depend on what the news was? On what happened in the world the day before it went to print? It's not our fault if last Saturday's was a bit dreary. Papers—well not since the early days of *The Daily Sport*—don't make up the news, they report it. "Guys, guys, listen, yesterday's Tsunami edition got us a huge spike in sales; quick, somebody blow up another continent. And that 'Diana Dies!' issue is still unbeaten. Quick, newshounds, one of you run over a princess. Oh, you already did that...."

But, now my news. Pavla has got a new job. Not with twins this time, but with two siblings nonetheless. The first is sixteen and could easily look after herself. What she isn't prepared to do, however, is look after her eleven-year-old sister. So the father— the mother ran off with an old flame whom she met on *Friends Reunited*—has hired Pavla essentially to pack them off to school in the morning, collect them in the afternoon, and hang around at my place the rest of the day.

She won't tell me this generous (aka useless) man's name for fear I will humiliate him in my column, but I can tell you his number plate is PGX 555Z, so if you have a mate who is a copper or in the DVLA, please email me at the paper. It's a Mercedes V Class People Carrier, which strikes me as a contradiction in terms. The cool of the Mercedes Marque is warmed up somewhat by the naff minibus nature of the model. Also any credit he gets for buying a family vehicle as opposed to a roadster, funky Beetle, or retro Mini is swiftly wiped out by the fact it is a seven-seater and his family (even if you include Pavla) only stretches to four. I ventured to Pavla that he might need the extra space for two Alaskan Malamutes, Giant Schnauzers, or whatever the latest fashionable breed is (apparently dog-in-a-basket is out of vogue and dog with its own postcode is in), but Pavla was tightlipped, and accused me of fishing for information with which to decorate this column.

Well, I have to write about something. Mary's pregnancy continues smoothly, Cressida is on an Antarctic cruise photographing penguins, and Adam is busy learning lines for *Guys and Dolls,* even though opening night is months away. He is under pressure because he knows Sigur the Icelandic stage manager has his eye on his part and so he doesn't want to give the Drama Society any excuse to sack him.

In conclusion, that doesn't leave much to write about. Therefore, Pavla's single-dad employer is all I have. It is August, after all, and unless there is another seasonal child kidnapping to obsess the media, the news is thin. I had heard about *Friends Reunited* breaking up marriages before (*Editor's Note: This is not the position of The Commentator or its owners, affiliates, or subsidiaries and is unsubstantiated and anecdotal.*), but never encountered a real life example. Despite my thrust back into the limelight, I still remain as out of date as the bubble perms that dominated the magazine covers in my salad days; Gilbert O'Sullivan, Leo Sayer, why have you not got in touch?

I suppose I could comment on the annual summer wildfire phenomenon, but the raging annual incineration of drought-and-wind-blasted tracts devastating parts of Spain, Greece, California, and Australia (in January, of course) is not exactly *new*. The only detail that does grab my attention during this regular occurrence is the ubiquitous use of the term "*wild*fire." Is this to imply there is such a thing as a *civilized*-fire? Perhaps akin to a civilized Nazi? "In a moment I will burn down all your property and *ze* land around it *unt* all your family will die of smoke inhalation…but first we must talk of Goethe, Haydn, and the plays of Friedrich Schiller…and do not fear, I will not burn your mahogany desk as it is a Ludwig Mies roll top and superb example of the *Bauhaus* school."

Hopefully, something more interesting will happen next week. However, unless they suddenly add a sixth Test to the Ashes series, I fear I shall have to return to the subject of Pavla's new employer. Still, maybe this is the calm before the storm…

FC Naylor

24. Saturday, August 12

No column was published this week either.

25. Saturday, August 19

Famous last words, eh? Well not as famous as "Kiss Me Hardy" or "Et tu Brute." How generous of Nelson and Caesar to focus their attention on their surviving friends at the moment of permanent eclipse. I expect to be far more self-involved on the cusp of my demise. Unlike some I could name, I have not planned my last words in advance, but not because I fear the obituary writers may devote more column inches critiquing the semiotic cargo of my final sentence than to the many pages of my life's published work (much like the opening batsman pilloried for that single misjudged moment of madness when he reverse-swept his wicket away on 99, rather than praised for scoring more runs in that inning than anyone else in the match, excluding extras). No, it is because I doubt very much these words will come out right. The intended pop culture reference, Latin quote, and clever inverting of Spinoza or Rousseau is most probably going to come out as garbled as Lord Goldsmith's legal advice on the invasion of Iraq. It will be like my ex-wife's birth plan, delicately designed to enable Toby to enter the world as gracefully, naturally, and independently as a blood-and-mucus-daubed infant feasibly can. Unfortunately, the diligently rehearsed, drug-free, doctor-absent shamanic chanting, sipping of Valerian root tea, and floating in a salt water-filled Tibetan Ku Dru, swiftly gave way to screams of, "More gas and air, now!" and "I've changed my mind, put me to sleep, and forcep the f***er out!".

"Events," as Harold Macmillan intimated, are the scourge of good planning. And in any "event," I imagine my final words to be less on the noble lines of Dickens', "It is a far, far better thing that I do now..." and more of a humongously indignant, "What do you mean there's *nothing more you can do*, Doctor?"

Anyhow, my prediction of a slow news month was contradicted by events to the extent that my column was bumped last week (I checked my contract to make sure I still got paid before cancelling my plans to sabotage the printing press.) because the space was needed for the extra coverage required by our financial editor (though for some reason, Super Summer Sudoku, Ortense Magellan's Summer Pudding Pull-Out Special, and the Johnston's Paint Trophy South first round fixture list all made the cut). It would appear the death rattle of capitalism is major news—not so to this writer who has been preparing for this inevitable result with no less anticipation than the 1999 Heaven's Gate Cult awaiting the Hale Bopp comet and its attendant space ship to airlift them free from the end of the world.

"Cycle of boom and bust...increasing the gap between the richest and poorest...rapid monopolization as the big financial institutions swallow the smaller ones..." you'd forgive me for thinking I was quoting a new translation of *The Grundrisse* rather than the Leader column of the favorite newspaper of the President of the Institute of Directors. If, after 9/11, we all became New Yorkers, looks like we are all Marxists now. Sadly, the mortality of the currently dominant arrangement of the means of production and exchange is being publicized more by capitalists than the communists who used to pray for its demise. The way I see it, credit drying up means gullible people can no longer borrow themselves into marriage-busting, nervous down-breaking debt; house prices falling means first-time buyers will no long drive their parents mad by having to move their girlfriends into their childhood bedrooms, but instead will be able to afford a place of their own without an ever-present dad travelling the house whistling *Bring Me Sunshine* ostentatiously loud to subtly warn them to put their clothes back on; meanwhile the global collapse in car sales and cancelling of holiday flights will solve traffic and air pollution problems overnight; and the shrinking of world economic output will make increasingly out-of-reach targets in carbon emission reductions a shoo-in. I just fail to see a downside.

As for the greedy, reckless, overpaid, tax-dodging parasites in the city losing their jobs…well not even Mexican drug lords, Ukrainian arms dealers, and Albanian human traffickers would want to see a single one of their daughters married to that lot. The only disappointment is that modern air conditioning prevents the upper reaches of the Gherkin and One Canada Square from having any windows that actually open, thus making the absence of pinstripes and body parts on the pavement the distinguishing difference between now and 1929.

No, I fear having to sell one's second bought-to-let home at slightly less something-for-nothing profit, not being able to borrow against one's equity to buy a new Aga, extend one's oak flooring up the walls and ceiling and into the garden, and a gradual slow down in converting communal property into private flats is probably as bad as it gets. Unless you are one of the those people who spent their working days trading in collateralized debt obligations, flogging credit default swaps, or short-selling bank stocks—in which case frittering away your bonuses surfing amputee porn on the Internet at home should provide opportunity for some long overdue edification.

Oh, and as for Pavla's no-news new boss, she only went and slept with him over the weekend!

FC Naylor

26. Saturday, August 26

I am still fighting for space with the ever-expanding "GLOBAL FINANCIAL CRISIS!" section of this paper. I cannot believe that for years this newspaper shook its head at surging house and oil prices with the same millenarian condemnation of Savonarola at the sinners dragging him to the stake. Yet, now as many prices finally fall, they are itemized with the gloom and *gravitas* of casualties at the Somme.

The financial sector, the heartbeat of capitalism, is facing tough government regulation and coming under democratic supervision. Bank executive salary caps will reduce inequality, public part-ownership of the banks means profits can go on school buses as well as yachts, plunging oil prices (from $147 to $47 a barrel) means the poor will be able to buy things and the elderly heat their homes. As for the massive government debt sparked by Keynesian borrowing, unemployment benefits bill, and a big drop in corporation and personal tax revenue forcing future cuts in public spending? Well, what better excuse to pull completely out of Iraq and Afghanistan, and not renewing Trident's nuclear missiles (dismissed by former Chief of the Army, Lord Bramall, as a Cold War creation utterly redundant today)? It is win, win. If it is not a case of Prime Minister Harold Macmillan's, "you never had it so good," it behooves me to quote our final Old Labour Prime Minister, Jim Callaghan, and conclude, "Crisis, What Crisis?" (How weird it is that being "Old Labor" in the twenty-first century is suddenly no longer as much fun as being a vegan at a fox hunt?)

Now, Alistair, can you please stop this hysterical over-reporting and give me my 1,000 words back, please?

FC Naylor

P.S. More good news—this financial *crisis* has cost Pavla's employer his job in the city so she is expecting to be let go, which means their affair should end. This joy has alleviated the pain of a rather headachy week.

27. Saturday, September 3

Curses! I am still on restricted wordage, but my shortest column (August 26) has received the largest numbers of complaints. Maybe if I finished this column now with this sentence I would beat *The Commentator's* record. The liberal media avoid complaints like a Medusa does mirrors, but I consider being complained about as being placed in very good company.

Can you guess what provoked the largest number of complaints about the BBC? Swearing? Blasphemy? *Jerry Springer: The Opera* had both in it, but still only comes second (with 55,000). No, the answer is when the BBC interrupted *The Antiques Roadshow* to broadcast live the release of Nelson Mandela. Yes, on February 11, 1990, Series 12, Episode 6 was briefly suspended and the image on our screens of Hugh Scully cradling an eighteenth century, ornamental ceramic Labrador was replaced with the African statesman of the century emerging from Victor Verster Prison to the thunderous echo of history turning a corner and the walls of apartheid falling down. The sequence was transmitted live across all six inhabited continents, but apparently did not go down so well in Horsham or Padbury, from whence the majority of complaining letters had their source. Probably from the same family. (I tell you, there's far more inbreeding in the Home Counties than in Pitcairn or Norfolk. The gentry are all related in the Shires, where you f**k horses for fun, and cousins for children.)

So, there's Brigadier Rupert Alabaster-Bollocks and his wife Lady Candida Range Rover Thrush Virus staring greedily at all the antiques being displayed on TV. "A chair! We've got some of them, might be worth a few bob…" when, "Oh, look, there's a black man! Hmm, possibly one of a pair. Don't get many round here, though. Candida!"

But Rupert's wife can't reply because she and their two daughters were probably all being shagged by Alan Clark at the time.

"This is outrageous, Candida! I fought in the war; well, I didn't actually fight, but people who worked for me fought in the war. Someone had to stay home and get those evacuees to work our land."

Rupert can't find any paper on which to write his indignant letter so he carves it in his footman's back.

"Dear BBC, The South African authorities have kept Mr. Mandela in custody for twenty-seven years…is it too much to ask that they hang on to him for another ten minutes 'til the end of the program?"

The complaints I received were of a different order. Allegedly, I have made light of the economic plight of the many innocent victims of the recession, for which I would have felt shame had they been referring to steelworkers from Sunderland or shop assistants from Woolworth's being unemployed or families having their houses repossessed. However, they weren't. My complainants are all employed, but very annoyed that interest rates have plummeted so low that the return on their bank savings is down, and more annoyed that market volatility has now made it really hard deciding where to invest the rest of their copious spare cash. I wrote back to every reader sympathizing and assuring him or her that I would take up the matter of the terrible burden of their surplus money and lobby my MP…to raise inheritance tax. After all, capital gains tax, corporation tax, and even personal tax is now so easily avoidable by putting your family on the payroll, getting yourself paid in never-to-be-honored loans from a chimerical trust fund based in Liechtenstein or a shell company in the Cayman Islands (which literally has more companies registered than people who live there and almost as many shell companies as shells), that inheritance tax is now the only way left to get the well-off to contribute *anything to anyone* other than the cost of skiing lessons to their kids' private school and commercial bribes to Saudi princes.

In addition, to make it doubly fun, inheritance tax can never be accused of being a disincentive to work because it doesn't tax earned wealth, it only taxes unearned wealth! Yes, while your mum and dad enjoyed living in their Georgian villa, or four-bedroom detached house; it gained in value without them having to do a single thing. Literally, just sitting around multiplied the value of their property by up to 1,000 percent if you bought in 1980 and sold in 2007. But, don't worry; they are not going to be allowed to gain from this most un-Christian Mammon-worship. No. They are going to die and the person who will gain is you! Yes, and you did even less than your mum and dad to get that squillion pound asset. You haven't lived there since you were a teenager, rarely visited because, well, life is simply soooooooo busy, you are going to sell it the day after you inherit it, and then write to me to complain you can't make up your mind where to invest the cash now that Bernie Madoff is in jail.

But, wait, £600,000 tax-free isn't enough. No, you want it to be *completely* tax-free. Except, hang on, earlier you were complaining that our government is in deficit having had to bail out all those debt-bundle-selling pyramid schemes commonly known as banks, so I should have the Treasury's ear when I suggest the only way to increase the tax yield in a year of contracting growth is…to tax you, dear reader, you.

That's the *good* news. The bad news is that Pavla has not ended her affair with her employer. Turns out the poor sacked soul's redundancy payment and final-salary pension is higher than her family's lifetime earnings and "The Boss" (not Bruce Springsteen) is using this opportunity to start a new life…with Pavla. Apparently he read my column describing his teenage children as being old enough to look after themselves and agreed. Well, actually, he agreed they were old enough to be looked after by their aunt. So, his sister is going to have to move in since he is moving out with Pavla. He is leaving the rat race (i.e., cashing in his share options and leaving his kids) and plans to travel, grow a beard, and have a lot of sex with Pavla.

I warned her that his midlife crisis would last only as long as the recession. As soon as employment and house prices go back up, he will dump her and return to his kids. And, I added, they are going to suffer doubly because, not only are they losing a dad, that house he has left them in is *so* going to be hit by my new inheritance tax policy, and those kids will get zilch! But, Pavla is having nothing of it. The older girl, Ophelia, has put down on Facebook as her principal hobbies *witchcraft* and *smoking*. The younger, Iphigenia, is on a pre-teen dating website, where she describes herself as *needy* and *callous* and that was in the "character *strengths*" section.

Well, this prompted me to ring Toby up and congratulate myself on finally getting confirmation I really am *not* the worst father in the world after all. Toby, of course, gets emotional, then Mary starts crying in the background, and the next thing I know they have booked flights out of JFK and we all have reservations at some fancy London restaurant. Adam turns up at my house in mid-phone-conversation with some radical new pain-killing medication that allows me to be both pain-free *and* operate heavy machinery at the same time, so I feel obliged to invite him along. I was hoping it would clash with one of his *Guys and Dolls* rehearsals, but the woman playing *Adelaide* went to a "Find Your Inner Voice" workshop and, after three hours of primal screaming, lost it. Everyone has the week off. Well, at least I should have plenty to talk about in next week's column.

FC Naylor

P.S. You may have noticed I have exceeded my reduced word count. I tried to talk to Alistair about this in advance, but he wouldn't return my calls, so I went ahead on my own. Apparently, Alistair has not been in his office much this last week. I know Cressida cut her Antarctic holiday short (A slice of melting glacier suddenly broke off the Larsen shelf threatening to hole the ship she was travelling on, ironically officially classified as an *Icebreaker,* presumably in the sense of the crew's ability to set at ease passengers meeting for the first time with some improvised games, rather than the solidity and sharpness of the vessel's prow.), so maybe she and Ali have decided they need to spend more time with each other.

28. Saturday, September 10

What a week on the domestic and work front. Turns out Alistair and Cressida were not celebrating their reunion after her sojourn in the land of the midday moon, but bunkered down with the Board. I knew something must be up when I popped in to Alistair's antechamber to see if receptionists Sonya and Michael were still an item. Well, if Pavla can go out with a man twice her age, why can't Sonya go out with someone twice her age (*closer to three times her age. Ed.*). As it turns out, Michael was on duty, so I chose not to raise the subject after all. What I did see, however, was Alistair's desk. *All* of his desk. In other words, that half-acre of mahogany previously covered by the architect's model of our riverside dream home, Parnell Palace, was no longer obscured. A quick word to a colleague from the financial pages—he owed me a favor after I sneaked him an experimental migraine treatment from the Ansdell Goodrich Lab (*The Commentator in no way condones the distribution of unlicensed drugs. Ed.*), and I discover that the office move is off!

Stairway Construction (Motto: "You dream it. We build it!" They obviously never worked for Hunter S. Thompson.) who were commissioned to develop the site cannot get any further credit from the besieged banks after the collapse in commercial property values. Meanwhile, all their big retail clients have cancelled their contracts due to an irreversible fall in predicted future sales, which makes a new mall in the city center about as profitable as a fetish club in a lamasery.

I attempted to raise the repercussions of this setback at my dinner *party* with Toby and Mary in a Japanese restaurant (chosen presumably because Nippon's GDP is even more arrested than ours) when Adam interrupted me in full rant. This event being more rare than a baby shower in the panda compound at London Zoo, I stopped to listen. Turns out his thespian ambitions, which I freely admit to have inflated myself, are now in jeopardy. That week-off allegedly due to his co-star's laryngitis was actually a ruse concocted by Sigur the SM to entrap my friend. Adelaide did not have trouble with her adenoids at all.

So, Adam missed three rehearsals including one with the full orchestra present and the director is now questioning his commitment. Sigur, one of whose jobs it is to contact actors who fail to turn up, is claiming Adam never returned his texts and it almost came to blows. I suggested to Adam that he present my last week's column as evidence of his integrity, but apparently *The Commentator* is newspaper *non-grata* at *The West Finchley Players* on account of our theatre critic, Dorothy Pace, having lambasted a previous production in Dorothy's previous incarnation as a local reporter for *The Ham and High*. She called their production of R. C. Sherriff's World War I drama, *Journey's End*, a "ninety minute vindication of Kaiser Wilhelm's expansionist foreign policy, the futile suffering of the audience in the theatre easily outmatching that of the troops in the trenches. So much so, that one longed for a stray shell or machine gun volley to consume the house and end the sapping monotony of the production whose final curtain, when it eventually fell, was welcomed by the ticket holders with easily as much rapture as conscripts did the armistice." Dorothy then signed off by cleverly sneering that the run would "surely be over by Christmas," which was a bit rich given it was only booked for four nights anyway.

At this point, Pavla (Yes, she read my column and subsequently bullied her way onto the sushi restaurant's guest list), who was nibbling nervously on some California Roll (Er, since when is California part of Japan? I thought all those WW2 Arkansas internment camps were about *stopping* the Yellow Peril annexing America's West Coast. Don't tell me that locking up all those law-abiding, Asian-Americans for three years failed!), flashed her customary anti-German barb, which always makes Adam uncomfortable—some sort of inherited survivor guilt, I think. Anyhow, my discussion topic of the Parnell Holdings became so much collateral damage.

I had to feign a wheezing fit in order to return myself to the center of attention, but must have been a little too plausible— clearly I am more engaging an actor than the mummers of N3. Mary started shouting to Toby to do something or else I would die without seeing my grandchild, and then she started panting really heavily. I don't know whether it was the sake or Pavla falling on her knees and praying to Saint Hedwig of Silesia, but I convinced myself that Mary's hyperventilation was her attempt at inducing my grandchild's premature birth and I started wheezing for real. A full-blown panic attack ensued, forcing Adam to frantically triage as Mary's blue lips, Pavla's hysterical supplications, and my airless cheeks competed for his medical attention. Only the Japanese waiters appeared undisturbed, no doubt putting our antics down to an overzealous ingestion of Wasabi, a schoolboy error.

The conclusion to this undignified episode is that Mary, who soon will not be allowed to fly anyway, has decided to have her baby in the UK, so that I may attend the birth! Apparently, Cressy has found space in her credit-crunch dominated diary to put up Toby and Mary for the next couple of months. All, allegedly, for my sake.

Forgive me if this sounds more like a diary entry than a column, but Adam insisted I rest after my anxiety attack and I have had little time to comment on current affairs. I shall simply throw this bone: The deserved sense of guilt and shame for their forefathers' deeds is of a level that it must be borne by (a minimum of) two subsequent generations, in order to expiate fully the sins committed by the nations of Germany and Japan. You may chew on that.

FC Naylor

29. Saturday, September 17

You readers have chosen the subject to be discussed this week. Not "*bourgeois* tapas dinner party gossip," as an old writer friend from the Revolutionary Communist Party described last week's edition of my column. Maybe so, but this is from a man who once claimed, in print, that Serbia's crimes against Bosnia were invented by ITV. (And, surely the Left ate tapas in the Spanish Civil War.) Still, at least it wasn't holocaust denial. To pre-empt accusations of anti-Semitism, I know that some maintain the word "holocaust" should be applied exclusively to the extermination of Jews in the mid-twentieth century, but I was taught by an old East End Jewish Communist friend (yes it may seem a cliché, but it is nevertheless true, Jews and Jazz have always been ever-present guests in the house of the British left) the preferred term for those wartime atrocities is the Hebrew, *Shoah*. And, lest I be accused of being anti-Islamic, I refer to the forced flight of Palestinians from their homeland using the Arabic word *Nakba*. And, for good measure, I like to call the WWI Ottoman campaign against Armenians *Genocide* (a word coined by Polish Jewish Scholar, Raphael Lemkin in 1944), although I whisper it quietly when visiting Istanbul to avoid a *Midnight Express* experience. This emphasis on nomenclature may come across as pedantic—actually, I hope it does—but this is because an ideologically loaded word has been used to describe *me* on account of words I chose to describe others.

This week for the first time in my professional writing career, someone wrote to my editor (Alistair has now covered the gap on his desk with a bust of Charles Darwin. Does that mean we are relocating to the Natural History Museum, the Galapagos Islands…?) to warn that they are going to report me to the police for being a *racist*. Yes, FC Naylor a *racist*! This would be for my remarks about Germans and Japanese last week.

First off, I would like to say that neither Germany nor Japan *is a race*, so we can put that to bed immediately. (The indigenous Burakumin ethnic group and the Ainu people, as well as any Chinese survivor of the Nanking massacre, might wish to comment on *Japanese* racism—and let's not even get started with the Germans.)

Secondly, identifying the racial status of individuals or groups being portrayed negatively, but *truthfully,* is not racist. Nearly all top sprinters and top heavyweight boxers have been black, while nearly all top golfers and top tennis players are white. Tiger Woods, the Williams sisters, and those giant Slavic Klitschko brothers are noteworthy, not just for their virtuosity, but for their counter-trend ethnicity. Most teenage knife and gun violence on English streets is committed by young black males, nearly all corporate tax evaders and serial killers are white adult men, while nearly all recent terrorists in the UK have been brown, and most of my favorite comedians are Jewish American. So, the question is, if a racial generalization is true, can it be racist?

When I say that a Londoner is far more likely to be stabbed to death on the High Street by a gangster, than an Israeli is to be blown up by an al-Qassam rocket fired by Hamas from Gaza, but that the Metropolitan Police didn't consider blanket bombing all our council estates as an appropriate response; is that racist, anti-working class, anti-Semitic? No. It's true, that's what it is.

I'll tell you what else is true and this is pretty momentous news. Contrary to general expectation, contrary to expert opinion, contrary even to my own Shaman-like foresight…I may outlive my column after all!

Now, I know what you're thinking (I am as I said, Shaman-like), but I am afraid no, this is not due to an intercessional miracle despite Pavla's entreaties, nor a post-Genome revolutionary drug therapy despite Adam's World Wide Web explorations. Neither am I in remission. In fact, my post-anxiety-attack tests have uncovered further reduced oxygenation in the blood and arrhythmia of the heart, all symptoms of advanced VHD to go along with the headaches. BUT…the newspaper may close down before I do. Quality print media often loses money, even more now the recession has meant advertising revenue is down (Murdoch wants to charge for *The Times* online content to prop up the paper version, the *Philadelphia Inquirer* and *Chicago Sun Times* have both gone bankrupt), and *The Commentator*'s circulation has been worse than mine for ages. But this time, Cressida will be hard pressed to persuade the Board to subsidize her loss-making favorite (i.e., her paper, not her husband). Apparently the whole Parnell Group has over-expanded and for the first time, the banks are refusing to reschedule their loans. As for those smart *Icelandic* investments…well we don't want to generalize about any more nations after offending the Germans and the Japanese, do we? Although the words *greedy*, *Lutheran*, and *whale eaters* come to mind.

So, see you next week—same time, same place. Maybe?

FC Naylor

(Editor's Note #1: Remarks concerning the financial future of the newspaper are published as comment and not fact.)

(Editor's Note #2: Mr. Naylor has not, as he seems to believe, been accused by a reader of being a "racist." He was actually accused of being a "rapist." In fact, everyone on our staff with a byline received the very same letter. A disgruntled, former employee is currently being questioned by police.)

30. Saturday, September 24

I was musing over the fall of capitalism while in Adam's waiting room, a little pissed off that he wouldn't make a home visit this week. "Need to be in the surgery to consult my records, FC," he purports. I don't understand quite why his records aren't portable, everything else is. Personally, I can't wait for all my biometric data to be loaded onto a single synthetic eyelash that can be read by a scanner. Adams says a number of his fellow GPs don't like the idea of a national database, as it endangers privacy. Well, the same thing was said about the Internet, the computer, the printing press, and I believe Tsai Lun (the first century eunuch who invented paper was frequently chased around the Louyang royal court by the chattering classes screaming that his record-keeping innovation would lead inexorably to a "Big Brother" state). He retorted that Eastern Han Emperor He was *already* acknowledged as a semi-divine feudal autocrat, and that if they had a beef with modernization, they should check out the charlatan who had just invented acupuncture! (Tsai Lun had handed over ten silver coins to "Doctor" Chang and yet his back was still killing him.)

As far I'm concerned, CCTV, IP address monitoring, vehicle registration recognition, and mobile phone call tracking is damn handy for catching criminals and, if they want my DNA, I'm more than happy to trade spit for security. You may think this odd of a socialist, but as far as I can see, the only reason to fear having all this recording going on is if you are: 1) a professional getaway driver, 2) an habitual kerb crawler, 3) a lying spouse who doesn't want the wife/husband knowing about you ringing the bookie/lover/dealer all the time, 4) a problem child not wanting his mum knowing how much time he spends on Facebook and YouTube, or 5) most likely, a rapist who doesn't want his sperm sample traced back to him.

By the way, I notice that the MP who shamefully was arrested for receiving government secrets from a Tory mole he planted in the Home Office—I say "shamefully" because at worst his crime was what, treason?—has successfully had the police destroy both his fingerprints and his DNA profile. I would check his pockets at the weekend for crowbars and/or Rohypnol.

As for those medical records, apart from those people falsely claiming invalidity benefits or concealing their heroin addiction, what is it everyone so needs to hide? As for the powers-that-be now having—scary, scary—a permanent record of yours truly's participation in demonstrations against nuclear weapons, the Vietnam War, internment in the Six Counties, the National Front, Apartheid, fitting up the Birmingham Six, the Special Patrol Group, cuts in the NHS, bombing Libya, sacking Wendy Savage, closing the pits, locking out the printers, sacking the Dockers, abolishing the GLC, Clause 28, Pinochet, the Poll Tax, fox hunting, the murder of Stephen Lawrence, and invading Iraq… May I remind you that very word "demonstration" is defined by the OED as "the action of making known"?

What would be the point of going if nobody knew you went? Where is the *demonstrating* in that? "Hey, guess what? Last night we managed to sneak out and march against Third World Debt *without anybody noticing*!" All that making a handy computerized national database available to everyone from the Chair of the Joint Intelligence and Security Committee to the Boots Pharmacist, from Interpol to Wilmslow Borough Council Parking Penalties Department will mean is that everyone can now find this stuff out at the simple pressing of a key. I could not be more grateful that my protests are finally to be preserved in this way and not washed away like so much beach sand by the twin crested waves of time and indifference.

And, after all, most young people, and many older ones, update their status with such reliable regularity and alert their friends to the latest posting of photos of themselves topless, stoned, or worse with such unprovoked alacrity, that private investigators and spies are rapidly joining giant tortoises and sub post offices as endangered species. Therefore, what is it that the privacy objectors are really worried might leak out?

The details of their bloody Swiss bank accounts is the answer, which brings me full circle to the fall of capitalism. Secrecy benefits the strong, not the weak. All this, I said, in Adam's waiting room as he searched for details of my white blood cell count. To be fair, as I proselytized about open government and shared knowledge, two anxious young people did slither away without keeping their appointments and I don't think it was to transfer their laundered millions from the British Virgin Islands to Liechtenstein; the man looked like he might have mental health concerns, for which he preferred discretion and the underage school girl might have been after private contraceptive advice. So, if I have unwittingly contributed to both a teenage pregnancy and a suicide, I apologize. (Speaking of secrets, I noticed that Adam keeps his *Guys and Dolls* costume at work and not at home. Hope you are reading, Esther.)

Anyhow, the economic conditions that consumed most of my visit to the surgery were prompted, not just by the Royal Bank of Scotland announcing the biggest losses in U.K. history (£40 billion before tax), but the latest "wealthy celebrity loses money invested in Ponzi scheme" sob story. (Can someone please answer me this? Given that all these movie stars, sports icons, and country club millionaires were already earning gazillions anyway, why did they feel the need to invest in Bernie Madoff's high-risk, high-yield funds in the first place? If you earn several million a year already, surely depositing your millions in a high street savings bank for a guaranteed 5 percent interest is going to see you alright. Is it essential to go for that unsustainable 10 percent return that smells more of fraud than Mickey Rourke does of vodka? No, you just gotta squeeze that extra few hundred grand a year on top. Next year's movie deal, five-season TV contract, record deal, dividend, salary, bonus, or profit is never enough.

And don't give me that, "I got a mortgage," bullshit. In fact, here's a solution you might want to consider if your mortgage is hurting you at several thousands of dollars per month—live in a smaller f***ing house!

Just as it is the fattest people, not the thinnest, who order the biggest portions, it is always the richest who most want more. The poor make do with a few quid on scratch cards. *You* bank your millions with a bloke whose auditor is his retired brother-in-law! Hello, alarm bells! As readers of *The Commentator,* you will of course want to know how this affects "The Arts" and I shall tell you.

Cressy has confessed she was hoping to surprise me by funding a proper production of my last play, but this has fallen victim to swingeing budget cuts. Well, I did write it when there were four million out of work in the U.K., maybe it should be revived now we are approaching that number again. (I have tried to make that day come sooner by recommending Alistair for redundancy to cut the newspaper's cost, but Cressy demurred. Not, Mr. Sinclair, because of her role as loving wife, but because of something arcane and punitively expensive to do with employment law, if I remember her words correctly.)

But, as concierges say of hotel lobbies, when one door opens, another closes. A patron has emerged! Not my Adam—he is on a fixed rate mortgage rather than a tracker, so he has not saved any money from falling interest rates. (Esther is furious.) Not Toby. He has his future family to think about…oh, and he has had to quit his job in order to come to the U.K. Not Cressy—see above. So who? Well, as you may have ascertained, I don't know many other people and it isn't my old Serbian apologist writer friend whom I mentioned last week. He is still paying damages to ITV.

It is someone Pavla knows and I meet him tonight. If the news about my hemoglobin proves better, then I might just have a new show!

FC Naylor

31. Saturday, October 1

The leaves are falling faster than my white blood cell count (but not as fast as shares in Lloyd's Banking Group or the England rugby team's world ranking), but my spirits are up. Last Saturday I was introduced to my new benefactor, a rare philanthropist in times of global recession. Apparently the only products whose sales *grow* during downturns are: 1) cigarettes, 2) chocolate, 3) alcohol, and 4) cinema tickets.

In addition, my mental picture of a drunken chain-smoker with a sticky brown moustache and 3D specs courtesy of Disney's *Up* at the Imax was not far wrong, except the specs were bifocals and the moustache was of hair. Even so, Pavla's associate was from Poland, where vodka, tobacco, and cartoons are a way of life. Fortunately, the 50 percent vegetable fat, 50 percent beet sugar 'chocolate' that dominates Eastern Europe has not made the journey to the U.K. where Organic Fair Trade bitter-as-sulphur seems to have annexed the national palette. I immediately thanked the man, Kristof Boniek (no relation to the Juventus dribbling legend), a rich businessman who makes his living importing…people. He runs an employment agency for low-skilled migrant workers. Although he hastened to add that he wasn't always a human trafficker; no, he originally made his fortune in…landmines. "Until your lousy Princess Di comes along…!" Kristof got out of the business after her intervention; the black market bribes drove down margins.

Now, you might think it hypocritical of me to do business with this man, but I do not see it as in the same league (no pun intended) as Manchester City taking money from Thaksin Shinawatra and then those Sunni Emirs from the Gulf. (Hell, my own QPR is owned by convicted fraudster and car crash choreographer, Flavio Briatore.)

However, I actually consider hypocrisy to be a badge of honor, for hypocrisy means practicing the opposite of what one preaches. I preach the overthrow of capitalist economics, not that it needs my help at the moment, and of imperialist politics. Yet, I take money from an employer who owns the means of production—the proprietor of this paper—although technically I think the banks now own it and the government owns them. I also watch American television programs, despite their country of origin being an exporter of illegal war, stress positions, and of waterboarding.

"Yeah, but everyone else colludes, too," you hear my excuse to be.

"And that makes you just as bad as everyone else!" you cry triumphantly.

No, it doesn't.

You see, the difference between everyone else and me is AT LEAST I PREACH AGAINST IT! Do you think supporters of colonial adventures and the exploitation of labor are better than me because they are *not* conflicted! Is war-profiteer and torturer-general Dick Cheney to be admired because his behavior was *consistent* with his beliefs, ergo he is better than me because he has *integrity*? Yes? Well, claw-hammering Peter Sutcliffe has integrity then because he sincerely believed there was nothing more fun than murdering random women…and acted on that belief! I think I would rather be a hypocrite and suck the polluted air because I need to live, and then with my next breath curse the environmental disregard of profit-led industry. Rather live with that hypocrisy than keep my honor intact and gas to death 2,000 residents of Bhopal and say, "Hey, don't criticize Union Carbide for negligence; it's okay…because we *sincerely* don't care!"

Unfortunately, I voiced this torrent of thoughts directly at Kristof, but luckily his English is pretty much limited to, "£2.00

per hour max," and, "You pay me now for room or I call Border Police," so it went over his head. You will be pleased to know that we did, however, manage to fall out later. I presumed he supported my work because of a nostalgic fondness for the General Jaruzelski martial law days of the 1980s. Back then, the only Western culture tolerated in Poland were translations of British Marxist sociology and episodes from the TV series *Triangle* (allegedly its frozen grey North Sea Ferry locations evoked in the good General, memories of childhood holidays on the Baltic). Compared to these, my leftwing, but idealist and non-totalitarian plays must have felt like Hollywood. I was wrong.

Pavla translated to me that Kristof's reason for sponsoring the show was that the NUM strike portrayed in my play reminded him of the Solidarnosc Trade Union rebellion in the ship works of Gdansk. I volunteered, perhaps gratuitously in retrospect, that I considered Solidarnosc leader, Lech Walesa, not as a liberator of the working class, but a power-hungry, Papist anti-Semite; and I mentioned the strong documentary evidence supporting accusations he was also a Communist Secret Service informant in the seventies (his Stalinesque moustache being a pretty big giveaway), as well as being behind Poland banning abortions in the nineties. At this point, Kristof tried to strike me—they don't pussyfoot around the terminally ill in Poland like we do—but, luckily, pluralist Pavla stepped in.

Anyhow (looking back, I suppose there *was* a clue as to Kristof's religious beliefs in his name), he quickly forgave me; we sat and ordered beer. His reasoning was that he has always maintained one is obliged to respect anyone who is frank and honest about what they believe in. In his words, he is prepared to share a drink with a person of any stripe as long as he is *not* a hypocrite.

And being, as you know, a hypocrite, I of course immediately agreed…

FC Naylor

32. Saturday, October 8

Auditions!

This takes me back. I remember when you actually got decent actors turning up to these things. Certainly had loads of *applicants* this time, but where are the audition pieces from Chekhov or Edward Bond, discussions about Bertolt Brecht or Barry Keefe, improvizations inspired by Ken Campbell or *The People Show*? Christ, I've seen more tapdancing this week than at all the *Virginia State Annual Bojangles Memorial Festivals* put together, more versions of Leona Lewis's *Bleeding Love* than a Billericay hen night on a karaoke riverboat, and every monologue that was not a transcript from *Skins* was from *Hollyoaks*. I want to punch Sylvia Young right in the face (*Mr. Naylor does not mean this literally—Ed.*), literally punch her. I don't care if she's a woman. Apart from all the close harmonizing teenagers whose only experience at the theatre seems to be *Joseph and his F***ing Technicolor Dreamcoat,* I wouldn't mind giving Lloyd Webber a bashing either (*This is not meant seriously—Ed.*). Seriously, stomp on his tiny deformed head.

As for the over-twenties, all the blokes' monologues were from *Lock, Stock, and Two Smoking Barrels.* Don't get me started on Guy Ritchie. I've never been a fan of Madonna, but during their divorce proceedings, I prayed to the Saints that she won custody of his child, Rocco, so she could eat him. (*This is a metaphor—Ed.*) Really eat him. And Guy would have to watch like Tamora, Queen of the Goths does with Chiron and Demetrius. Oh, no, that would make me Titus Andronicus!

As for the older actresses—much more experienced, some very talented…and every single one completely bonkers. How could I forget how mad actresses are? I swear that Peter Brook's *Marat-Sade,* in which all the characters are lunatic inmates putting on a play in a sort of French Bedlam, was based on the audition process for his RSC production of *Midsummer Night's Dream.* No wonder his *Mahabharata* was nine hours long. The longer the play, the longer the gap before you have to audition for the next one.

There was one chap I did like. Untainted by all those prescriptive voice workshops, genuine South Yorkshire accent, look of a real laborer—that's because he was one. Only performing he had ever done was historical re-enactments – *Sealed Knot* and all that, holding a pike and wearing a bascinet, running around fields recreating the Battle of Marston Moor. They call it harmless fun, routing Cavaliers or getting General Lee to sound the retreat from Gettysburg, but there were 8,000 dead and 20,000 wounded or crippled at the real Gettysburg. Compared to all that, *Grand Theft Auto 2* is nothing more than raised voices at a tea party. *And,* on the videogame you don't actually interact with real people.

Of course, these re-enactors only get away with simulating such carnage because Bunker Hill or Naseby sound all "Olde Worlde," and people use phrases like "goodly" and "Prithee," so you can convince yourself you are experiencing history. I say that if you are really interested in empathizing with the warriors of the past battles, re-enact something more contemporary like *Riot on Broadwater Farm Estate* or better still, *Fallujah 2006* with phrases like, "Die, raghead mother-f***er!" and "Merciful Prophet—peace be upon him—my eyes are boiling in my sockets! Karim, I thought you said they wouldn't use white phosphorus because it was against international law."

Or, they could stay historical and do *Stalingrad.* "Right, everybody, we're almost cast, but we still need one female re-enactor to play 'older Russian victim of SS gang rape'…no costume needed, luckily; plus, someone to play 'Soviet officer who turns guns on own retreating troops.' Lenny, who normally plays him, is rehearsing his 'Third Corpse-Mutilator' for next week's *Battle of Nanking*."

Light bondage and some spanking is *harmless fun* about power relations. Re-enacting the Crusaders blinding the Cathars of Beziers or eating Muslim children at Ma'arra is not.

So, disappointed with the quality of the auditioned, I asked Kristof to approach Daniel Day Lewis; he was unavailable building cabinets somewhere. Now Pavla is having conversations with Christopher Eccleston's people, though quite why she thinks that floppy-haired Bill Wyman of Formula One would wish to launch an acting career at his stage of life escapes me. Later Adam explained that *Bernie* Ecclestone is the Grand Prix midget mogul who claimed, "Hitler wasn't all bad"; *Christopher* Eccleston is the actor who used to play Doctor Who.

I was not particularly relieved, to be fair. Why swap the part of a time travelling super hero who lives in a Tardis for that of an emphysemic miner on hunger strike at the bottom of an abandoned shaft? I don't understand. But, apparently, Adam explained further, it is precisely that Jude-like suffering that has attracted the actor. (Although his people made clear that he gets a chauffeured car to take him to and from rehearsals or the deal is off.)

The only bad news is that blinking opening night is on Friday, December 2. This clashes with *Guys and Dolls*, so I will miss Adam's debut (He won his feud with the stage manager after getting the BMA to threaten not to refill Sigur's asthma prescription.) and Adam will miss my comeback! (Adam, with whom I roomed at University, did the lights for my first amateur foray into theatre, a one-act psychodrama called, if my memory serves me, *One Act Psychodrama*.)

FC Naylor

33. Saturday, October 15

No column was published this week.

34. Saturday, October 22

Well, last week's edition was fun, wasn't it? All seven sections were sponsored by the government of the Kingdom of Saudi Arabia. I know times are hard for *The Commentator* but this week's little revenue stream strikes me as contaminated as a milkshake on Mururoa Atoll. In order to save money, the editor accepted a treasure chest of Riyals from dear old King Abdullah, in exchange for his press secretary guest editing the entire Saturday edition. A bit like when *The Observer Magazine* is handed over to someone like Stella McCartney, only without any pictures because Sulaiman bin Aziz is a strict Wahabbi and considers the pictorial representation of any living creature blasphemous (let alone half-naked models)…which made the color supplement a bit shitty.

Apparently, it was the only way to keep the presses running while Cressida continues negotiating rescheduling company debts with the banks. Despite the price of oil dropping faster than the severed hands of a thief onto the sand in Riyadh's Square of Justice, the desert fiefdom of this remarkable family is pretty much inured against the bursting of the credit bubble and so was a useful refuge in these days of restricted choice. It appears the Burmese junta was too busy scaring up Karen tribesmen and Conrad Black's current address is Prisoner 18330-424, Federal Correctional Complex, Coleman, Florida. Anyhow, my column was surplus to requirements. (No, I am not dead, yet.)

Meanwhile, Cressida is begging for a loan from Barclays (no point talking to the Icelandic banks unless you like literature that's been on a downhill course since *Njal's Saga* came out in the thirteenth century—hey, and you thought our BBC2 was past its sell-by-date). However, Barclays won't bite because I slagged them off over their multi-billion dollar tax avoidance scheme *Project Knight*. Interesting choice of title for an *avoidance* scheme—*Project Knight*. It conjures images of Sir Gawain declining the challenge of the Green Knight, Galahad ignoring the Holy Grail, and Lancelot not returning Guinevere's calls. Why? Because they are too busy re-routing the King's coin through the Exchequer of the Burgundian court via the Angevin Bourse before ultimately depositing it offshore on the island of Avalon, presumably with its lack of obligation-to-disclose regulation.

Of course, there is nothing new about such New Speak. The American invasion of Iraq in 2003 was called *Operation Infinite Justice*. Agreed, it did eventually change its name (to the marginally less bombastic *Operation Enduring Freedom)*, but not because there was *not one* WMD (that's as in *Weapon of Mass Destruction*, not the rust-colored Vodka-based Alcopop, although you'd be hard pressed to find one of those in Baghdad either). No, apparently, "Infinite Justice" is what several faiths, including Islam, call God. That was considered insensitive even by the word-challenged George W. Bush, who approved the waterboarding of terrorist suspects, assuming it was some sort of Californian extreme surfing. "Hey, if the CIA wants to take them to the beach, heck, why not? It must get awful cramped down there in Camp Delta." (*Camp Delta* was itself renamed from *Camp X-ray* when solid walls replaced the chain link cages, in one example of re-decoration not to have been pioneered first on *Changing Rooms.)*

Moreover, it is not just financial institutions and foreign governments who mask their intent with dodgy labels that make "Guinness is good for you," (ironically brewed in Ireland, which has the lowest life expectancy in Western Europe) a paragon of understatement. The Metropolitan Police's anti-rape unit is called *Sapphire*. Why? Because women are partial to jewelry? After the 1980s extraterrestrial TV detective played by Joanna Lumley? And why is the Met's investigation of black-on-black crime called

Operation *Trident*? Has anyone in London ever been killed with a trident? Don't these murders typically involve a street gang wielding knives, or Hoodies with pistols speeding away from nightclubs in cars? Rather than the last scene of *Thunderball,* with frogmen in aqualungs chasing each other with spearguns.

Some euphemisms I understand. Cassius Clay repudiated his slave name to become Muhammad Ali. Dandelion Richards became plain "Angela" to undo the damage done by her psychotropic parents, Keith Richards and Anita Pallenberg. (Though fellow rock heiress, Diva Thin Muffin Zappa, felt no such urge. I guess with a crazy surname like Zappa, in for a penny....) My own son Toby and his previous ever-dieting girlfriend Breeze (so called presumably because that is all it takes to push her over), dreamed of having a child called Allegra (after the stalwart Austin car?) and now that he is actually going to sire a son, he is going to be named after me, even though, to this day, only my ex-wife and the two drunken German sex tourists who witnessed our Bali wedding have even half heard for what FC stands. She was too out-of-it to remember and they are both serving ten years for offending public decency in Singapore, which is why, to honor my commitment to telling it how it is, I can now reveal my full name to the world.

F***ing C**t Naylor

P.S. In consequence of this paper being temporarily funded by a hereditary absolute monarchy, I have donated half of this week's fee to Amnesty International toward improving the living conditions of prisoners kept incarcerated in Saudi jails. The other half will go to whichever incarcerated gang banger in Coleman Prison first makes Conrad Black his special friend.

35. Saturday, October 29

Got many letters, although I think most of them were by Barbara Amiel, for libellng her husband and doing so because of my anti-Semitism, which is very odd because Conrad Black isn't Jewish, but he was once the owner of *The Jerusalem Post.* On the other hand, I once bought two Jaffa oranges and a VHS ex-rental copy of *Lemon Popsicle,* so I guess that makes me Jewish, too. Weird idea, unless you adhere to some contemporary secular version of transubstantiation, whereby a person *literally assumes* the nationality of his possessions, which is difficult should you happen to simultaneously be in possession of objects from different nations, such as clothes. By that reckoning, my feet would be Italian (Thank you for the Ecco sandals, Cressida.), my legs American, my torso Chinese, and my genitals would appear to be from Malaysia. And, if you include food…well then at all costs avoid the buffet at the Commonwealth Institute or you will be struck by global schizophrenia. Ergo, disapproving of Conrad Black is not anti-Semitic; it's simply common sense.

Paradoxically, I simultaneously got letters for being anti-Islamic because of my comments regarding the House of Saud (not a clothes shop on Oxford Street, though I think they own a few). And, yet, I specifically did not call into question their religious beliefs, their authoritarian politics, ideological censorship, or violent judicial policies. However, as it happens, I do not like Islam.

That's right, I don't. Most of my friends will pretend they do and claim they just don't like *extremism*. I'm different. I'll tell you straight, I don't like moderate Islam either, and for my Jewish readers, I must add I don't like Israel to boot. Confused? What am I, an anti-Arab Nazi perhaps? No, I don't like Nazis either or racists. In fact, I think the answer to a BNP march is not a Council ban on the grounds of public order, but a good kicking. Sod their civil rights. The truth is, I don't approve of any religion and will never approve of a religious state, be it Jewish like Israel, Muslim like Iran or Mauritania, or Christian like the United Kingdom. (Yes, our Head of State is automatically Head of the Church of England, which makes us a religious state, even though most British people don't give two hoots about religion.)

I believe citizenship on the basis of religion is wrong. Legislating against private adult consensual sexual practice on the grounds of religion is wrong. Persecuting unbelievers is wrong. Holding the laws of God above those of man is wrong because secular legislation is mandated by democratic vote and subject to recall, but the legitimacy of divine rule is not permitted ever to be contested whatever the circumstances are and whatever the size of the majority wishing to do so. Law must by definition be both binding and subject to amendment or revocation on the basis of social consent, yet one is not allowed to question the Law of the Book or adapt it to fit changes to social mores or the physical environment. The content of a law must be discussed and its relevance and justness backed up by argument. Content should also be its provenance, not its inclusion or absence in some revered book of the past alleged to be holy, whether it be the *Bible*, the *Koran*, the *Veda*, the *Tao Te Ching*, the *Watchtower*, the *Zohar of Moses de Leon*, Joseph Smith's *Golden Plates*, L. Ron Hubbard's *Battlefield Earth: A Saga of the Year 3000*, Aleister Crowley's *A Magick in Theory and Practice* (That doped up old goat couldn't even spell magic or his own name, for that matter; it's Alistair not Aleister—twat.), a post-it note on the dashboard of one of the Bhagwan Shree Rashneesh's '93 Rolls-Royces, Mystic Meg's tea leaves, Derek Acorah's spirit guide Sam, the placard of the "Eat Less Protein" man of Piccadilly Circus, the entrails of Papa

Shango's disembowelled chicken, the Dreamtime, Happy Hunting Grounds, Hari Krishna, Hari, Hari, I'm a teapot!

God does not exist and even if he did, that would not entail a duty to worship h/Him. Christ did not turn water into wine, five fish into fifty, or raise the dead. There is no big-eared half-elephant/half-man or multiple-armed lady warrior god or goddess. That is simply deranged; a cow is a cow, a pig is a pig, and Gabriel did not whisper in the ears of the Messenger or the Virgin Mary. The Shahid will not be welcomed by a garden paradise full of virgins, bad people do not come back as termites (If reincarnation were true, which means every living creature is a karmic copy of a previous living thing, the population figure would have to be forever static, instead it is ballooning.), and as I have explained before, one is not compelled to respect other people's beliefs simply because they are sincerely held. (See column 31 above.)

You sincerely believe God created the world in 4004 B.C. and there were dinosaurs on the Ark? I sincerely believe you are an idiot. You claim God wants you to stone to death women who commit adultery. I think you are full of ignorance and hatred. You reckon the Emperor of Japan is a direct descendant of the sun goddess Amaterasu Omikamo or that the Dalai Lama is the reincarnation of Avalokitesvara, the thousand-armed Buddhist master; I think you have been at the sake/fermented Yak's milk. If one had to respect all sincerely held beliefs, you would have to respect David Icke, Erich von Daniken, Charles Manson, and the delusions of my schizophrenic friend Mac who once told me completely straight-faced the Sea Devils out of Doctor Who once followed him down Kensington High Street. You would have to respect the verdict of the Los Angeles County Court trial that acquitted O. J. Simpson and respect the passionately held assessment of Sir Alex Ferguson that Manchester United was the better team when they lost 4-1 at home to Liverpool! Strength of conviction does not earn respect, quality of idea does.

In other news, Eccleston is in! His proposed film about the trial, torture, and execution of fifteenth century revolutionary Florentine preacher, Girolamo Savonarola, hit a blip when its potential investors concluded they did not want to make a film about the trial, torture, and execution of fifteenth-century revolutionary Florentine preacher, Girolamo Savonarola because nobody wanted to see a film about the trial, torture, and execution of fifteenth-century revolutionary Florentine preacher, Girolamo Savonarola.

So, Eccleston has a gap in his diary and will play the part of Underwood the miner in *Lamplight*.

FC Naylor

P.S. Although I do not like Conrad Black, who is not Jewish, I also do not like his wife, Barbara Amiel, who is Jewish, but not because she is Jewish, because she is Barbara Amiel.

36. Saturday, November 5

Today is Guy Fawkes Day. For some, this is a celebration of the saving of democracy since the Houses of Parliament were saved in the nick of time from being blown up. However, given that Britain's Parliament in 1605 was about as democratic as a Taliban Jirga in North Waziristan—no women, no young people, no voting—that claim is as stretched as Al Gore's claim to have invented the Internet. What November 5 actually celebrates is the torture, hanging, drawing, and quartering of rebellious Roman Catholic, Guido Fawkes, after his arrest for treason. The hanging was sufficient to choke and scar its victim, but not to kill, so that the victim is conscious for the quartering procedure. That involves cutting off the man's penis and testicles, as well as ripping open his stomach and tearing out his intestines. These are then burnt in front of his face before his head is chopped off, and then his limbs and various parts hung from gibbets pour *encourager les autres*. So, next time you see a lifelike effigy on a bonfire on Guy Fawkes Day, be sure to point out the mistake and complain, "No, no, no. Only his cock, balls, and guts were burnt, not the rest of him!" I did this once, was arrested, and threatened with being put on the Sex Offenders Register for using inappropriate language in front of children; Children who were playing with Catherine wheels! These are fireworks named after St. Catherine of Alexandria, who was being broken on a wheel (her arms and legs, sequentially shattered by blows from a cudgel) before her bonds miraculously became undone. Not the best of all God's miracles, since she was immediately beheaded instead, but hey, ho. I say put those gruesome party organizers on a register.

Catherine was executed (aka judicially murdered), simply for being a Christian in the fourth century, which brings me onto the third meaning of Guy Fawkes Day. Now I am no fan of child molesting, Nazi appeasing, or no-women-allowed religious hierarchies, but I can think of other ways for Englishmen to express disapproval of the Vatican. Somehow, the same people who were horrified when some hot-headed young Muslims burnt copies of *The Satanic Verses* on the pavements of Bradford seem to think it crosses the line to burn books, but immolation of replica humans is to be cheered—bring the kids and the toffee apples! But then anti-Catholic sentiment has been part of the folklore of this country for centuries, and for every Gerry Adams or Martin McGuiness walking the path of reconciliation, there is a sanctimonious Tony Blair whose Christian God guided him to war. In his defense, that infamous Iraqi WMD dossier was so well sexed-up that even the Omniscient One might have been fooled into believing there were mobile biological labs scooting around the desert like drug-peddling ice-cream vans on a Dewsbury housing estate.

By the way, have you noticed that the editors of *The Commentator* are so wrapped up in organizing management buyouts, ring-fencing their final salary pension schemes, and updating their CVs they have no time to bowdlerize my copy. (That's "Bowdler" as in the English Regency prison reformer who also published expurgated family versions of Shakespeare and not "disemboweller" as in "hanged, drawn, and quartered.") There has been no editorial censorship for a while and, subsequently, last week's column elicited a succulent menu of complaints. Many came from predictable sources—a glossy brochure sent by the Osho International Meditation Resort in Pune, a polite letter from the Public Relations Department of The International Society of Krishna Consciousness, a copy of the Zohar (Wasn't that the name of some hairdresser/spy in an Adam Sandler movie?) from London Kabbalah, an invitation to a Black Mass from The Surrey and Kent Satanic Guild with a promise that Marianne Faithful would be there, naked (I think this might be a spoof, but I kept the photo anyway.), a visit from two very nice American men in suits from Salt Lake City (Thank you for the advice, Chad and Sherman.), followed by a visit from two very nice black ladies from the Jehovah's Witnesses (Thank you for the biscuits, Blessing and Eunice.), a chicken head from Voodoo Warriors (I think they might actually be a band rather than a cult.), some red string from Madonna, and nothing actually material from Derek Acorah; however, my curtains and a cereal bowl on the breakfast bar appeared to wobble unaccountably late last night.

And, for those of you interested, preparations have started on *Lamplight*. A designer is fabricating the pit head set, the actors are learning their lines, and the director, Remy, has already banned me from rehearsals. He has also cottoned on to the idea that the main character is called "Underwood," and that coal is essentially carbonized wood underground and wants to highlight this word-play by carving the main character's face into a chalk escarpment above the pit head to show he is literally *of the earth* in which he works. I teased lightly that it sounded like *Pilgrims Progress* meets Mount Rushmore. He said in his *Rive Gauche* accent, "Yes, but does Gutzon Borglum's Mount Rushmore come with a live Balinese Gamelan Orchestra?" and kissed me. I replied that my sarcasm must have got lost in translation and had he been inside the Bloomsbury Theatre yet? Not exactly the O2 Arena! He dismissed that and mentioned his work in Europe with *Archaos* and *Cirque du Soleil* and in England with *Aylesbury Youth Detention Centre*, and how he wants to concentrate on "physicality, rhythm, and tone." I suggested he might prefer to concentrate on "acting, the script, and facing the audience." So, I am banned now.

This is annoying because as a writer, I need to make sure the words I wrote on the page will sound right in the mouths of the actors. I need to be on set to continuously polish the dialogue. I can only do that by listening to it being said out loud. Luckily, Adam, who asserts it would have been too knackering for me to commute to rehearsals every day anyhow, has volunteered to repeatedly read the script out aloud to me in my flat so I can review and re-write. Then he will drop off my re-writes at the rehearsal space. (Adam seems less and less available to his patients these days. I hope they are not being killed by some Agency-harvested, under-qualified, German locum.)

I took up his offer, since the alternative—getting Pavla to complain to Kristof about this over-educated (Who the hell is able to name-check the bleeding sculptor of the five presidents without having to Google it first? This man should be compiling crosswords, not directing plays.) and pretentious maniac. But, 1) Kristof has been remanded in custody for national insurance fraud, and 2) Pavla has been mysteriously absent from her flat upstairs in recent weeks.

FC Naylor

P.S. The name "Underwood" only came to mind as I was looking at an old Wisden Almanac and came across my favorite cricketer as a young man, the England and Kent left arm spinner, "Deadly Derek" Underwood. Of course, that was before he took the King's Rand and toured apartheid South Africa. But as a man of Kent, like myself (we were both born in Bromley), and having single-handedly squared the Ashes series with those incredible four last wickets against the Aussies back in 1968, I may not be able to forgive him, but I can't forget him either. I do wonder, had I named the miner after my second favorite cricketer, Ian Botham, if the director would have been equally literal and proposed painting a giant arse on the backdrop.

37. Saturday, November 12

The mystery of Pavla's disappearance has been solved. The subtle clue that only my Holmesian (shrewd Sherlock, not corpulent Eamon) super-brain could have successfully interpreted was the large diamond on the ring finger of her left hand. Well, after she backed that up with the words, "Look, FC, Clive has proposed to me." Yes, "beardy-man"—I shall not repeat his registered name again—beardy man has wangled a divorce quicker than Peter and Katie's on the grounds of his wife's many years of absence, and then popped the question to Pavla that same afternoon. Of course, I told Pavla that she did not *need* to marry to stay in the country because Poland is now in the EU. She replied that was not the reason she had said yes. So, I added that if it was money she needed, that I had made my will out to her. (Toby and the new grand kid won't need it; Mary's family of mineral magnates responsible for half the tar sands in Canada are almost as rich as Cressida.) Pavla started crying; with gratitude, I think, which was quite unnecessary seeing as my estate is absolutely valueless—I live in Council accommodation for which Cressida pays the rent, have no savings, own no equity or bonds, and royalties from my work are non-existent. So, being sole beneficiary of my will means nothing at all! On second thought, maybe *that w*as the reason she started to cry.

So, I pulled out the big gun. "If you are dreaming of an old-fashioned wedding in a fancy church, well your hubby-to-be is a divorcee and you are a Roman Catholic, so you can't have that either!"

Then she started gibbering in Polish and I gave up. Well, whatever it was she was saying, that bloke is clearly not good enough for her. Finally, after calming her down with tea (It really is a universal balm, isn't it? Especially when laced with the unlicensed sedative Adam procures for me for my recent anxiety attacks. I would have used vodka, but Pavla would have tasted it and I know these days rapists and hospital consultants are the only ones spiking young women's drinks, but my intentions were honorable.) I went through the motions and asked if they had set a date and was aghast when she replied yes, next bloody week in the frigging Polish Embassy where you do not have to wait for bans to be read. Why is mid-life crisis beardy-man in such a hurry? Is Pavla pregnant? Does anyone still care if a baby is born out of wedlock these days (outside Nicaragua and rural Pakistan)? Even if they do, Pavla must have several months to go, surely?

I knew a woman once whose husband traded her in for a younger, stupider model while the wife was pregnant by him. The child was born in the weeks between the Decree Nisi and Decree Absolute, making its legitimacy status most contentious. (Legally, the marriage remains extant until the Decree Absolute, but the purpose of the Decree Nisi is to set the date at which the marriage dissolves "unless a reason arises in between for it not to go ahead." You are then compelled to wait a couple of weeks to give that a chance to happen so you can tell the court and cancel proceedings.) Well, I would have thought that *the divorcing couple producing a baby* might qualify as a pretty good reason, no? However, the court was not told so the Decree Absolute was signed. I posed to my friend that in the absence of that clearly relevant information (the birth) being given to the Family Court, the Decree Absolute was arguably invalid and her current marriage to the new love of her life bigamous on the grounds she was still married to "the bastard who stole the best years of her life." Oh, and that meant that half her house was her ex's, too. I considered this an enthralling juridical conundrum and was up for a fascinating Socratic debate on the subject when the woman burst into tears and her new (faux) husband threw me out. If only

I had been on these not-even-available-on-the-Internet sedatives back then, I might have been able to salvage the situation. Alas…

Anyhow, my point is that whether it be a beer-bellied, balding banker from Basingstoke enticing a beautiful Thai virgin from Chiang Mai into the marital bed on the promise of a win/win situation of more financial security and fewer military coups, or a middle-aged American divorcee using her settlement to entice a young male Caribbean islander, or merely two people of the same race, class, and nationality getting it on, who is to say who is exploiting whom? All marriages are transactions, contracts that involve an arrangement of duties to the mutual satisfaction of both parties. Yet, other mutual personal arrangements we do determine as exploitation. We accuse *dealers* of exploiting their addict customers *to* whom they supply drugs, we accuse the *customers* of exploiting the prostitutes *from* whom they are supplied sex; opposite moral judgements drawn from two examples of an identical financial relationship, that of the exchange of physical pleasure for money.

Moreover, is a middle-class, white user being exploited by his black working-class drug dealer, or the other way around? Is the $2,000 per night escort being exploited by the lonely/horny executive, or vice versa? What of the female dominatrix and her submissive male clients? What is the power relationship there? There are those who say all wage labor is prostitution and, therefore, exploitative. Meanwhile, the English Collective of Prostitutes, the Trades Union for hookers says that they are not being exploited, but some feminists say they are. And would not the Bangladeshi sweatshop workers who stitch footballs for Western kids to kick about be even poorer without such an export market? They would probably live a subsistence existence fishing and farming on the delta at the mercy of floods and cyclones.

To close this circle of reasoning, some say all marriage is prostitution because the husband commonly has more social power and economic funds, while the wife is not permitted to deny him sex. (Except that common law has recently changed in this country so now she can.) On the other hand, one could say that wives exploit their husbands, living off their wages and using them like horses at stud to produce babies, which most men aren't really bothered about having, except that it was part of the deal. Deal, bargain, contract—it's all economics at the end of the day.

All the above I said to Pavla after she proudly showed me her ring. Thank goodness the super intense benzodiazepine derivative had addled her brain and she couldn't take it all in because when she finally interrupted my stream of consciousness (There's a reason Molly Bloom had hers on the toilet.), she finally whispered,

"I said yes, and requested we marry as soon as possible because I want *you* to give me away, FC. My father passed away when he was your age; so I would like you to…how you say…walk me down the aisle. Would you?"

And, because I was far too overcome to answer at the time, Pavla, this week's column is, I suppose, my way of saying yes.

FC Naylor

P.S. This meditation on exploitation raises once again in my mind that *fin de (vengtieme) siècle* cultural phenomenon, Reality TV. Does television exploit its participants? Is the spectacle of the uneducated, underclass morons flattered into confessing their sins, a modern-day Spanish Inquisition with Jeremy Kyle as Torquemada-lite? Are the performing monkeys on *Big Brother* naïve amateurs seduced by the temptations of fame being proffered banana-like by cunning expert professional keepers? Are the celebrities-on-the-slide whisked off to jungles and islands, fat camps and boot camps so desperate (to survive in an industry which looks after losers with all the compassion with which Dr. Harold Shipman looked after the elderly) they will easily trade dignity for dollars, victims of exploitation or merely their own vanity? Is the joke rather on the viewer who is watching bare flesh being sold as the finest of fashion? Or, is Reality TV the Bedlam of the twenty-first century and we the prurient voyeurs of other people's fallibility? And, are the self-admitted, broken-down addicts to alcohol and drugs like the slurring Osbornes, the suicidal Anna Nicole Smith, the coke-and-debt fuelled Kerry Katona exploiting the media to fund their excesses (and excessive sense of self-importance), or are they puppets on someone else's strings?

Fly-on-the-wall is so apt, isn't it, for this sort of television (and magazine, podcast, and newspaper spin-offs). Everyone knows flies live off other people's shit. And, if you still can't answer my questions, then do what FBI agent Mark Felt, in his guise as *Deep Throat* (Pornography—there's another convoluted matrix of exploitations in which the gawped-at women earn an average of ten times more than the men) advised Woodward and Bernstein to do during Watergate—follow the money. Find out who is getting rich off this.

Question: Who lives in the prestigious riverside properties of Bedfordshire and owns chalets in Biarritz, hold lucrative share options and health insurance, and live in stable families with children at private schools? Is it that bloke who used to be in Eastenders, the ex-model out of rehab, the singer from that boy band, the TV actor from the eighties, the Portuguese transsexual, or Greedy Mo? Answer: Well here's a clue. "Endemol" is Dutch for Satan.

P.P.S. Adam has been reading out loud to me Underwood's main speeches from *Lamplight*—long and rambling and forever going off on a spiral of tangents (Can tangents spiral? Whirl, perhaps? Gyre?). Only a theatre producer with English as a second language could possibly have agreed to produce this mess! I had no idea my clauses were so jumbled, piled on one another like the most long-winded paragraphs of Henry James after being ambushed by an earthquake...and so many postscripts! I have already begun the process of rewriting my play.

P.P.P.S. I thank the heavens that my policy is never to re-read these columns.

38. Saturday, November 19

What a busy week! I went out twice, and both times… in a taxi!

So, more to report on than ever. For starters, everybody's salary at the paper has been delayed a week. *I* don't care—I haven't paid a bill since my diagnosis; the bailiffs will have to drag my coffin into court. However, as a result of this financial freeze, my sub-editor has left and taken up a job on a lads' magazine called *Wank*—notice the lack of profanity-asterisks? That's proof (pun intended) that "Subbie" is here no more. And, for proof that we no longer employ a fact-checker either—there is no lads' mag called *Wank*. I made it up.

However, he genuinely has moved to some *muff and motors* publication whose name I simply can't be asked to remember (*Loser? Monkey Spank?*). Anyway, that publication can't guarantee him wages either, because all the print media are in such trouble but, to quote his Jerry Maguire-style walk-out words, "If I'm not going to get paid, at least this way I will be not getting paid up close to lots of topless totty off Hollyoaks." Give that man a Pulitzer.

Personally, I cannot see why anyone would be prepared to sacrifice anything simply to spend time with some semi-nude, young model/actresses from Chester. Not because of the inherent sexism. The accent. It's the same with the ubiquitous Cheryl Cole who's from Newcastle. Beautiful lady, but the minute she opens her mouth to speak, my God it's like falling out of the arms of

Ava Gardner and into those of Edna Everage—the face of Jackie Bouvier, the voice of Jackie Milburn.

By the way, my old sparring partner, the food critic, Ferdinand D'Arby, has withdrawn his labor in protest at his deferred remuneration, so I now have extra space, previously reserved for his New England butternut squash, sheared Piemontese truffle, and gruyere gratin.

Okay, taxi trip number one was to hospital—and this time not for my own health. Adam took a few days off from rehearsing *Guys and Dolls* and left his patients in the hands of his trusty receptionist (that Locum has been struck off and is now a successful telephone Psychic Counselor) and flew to America. By the way, Eccleston, I hear, is very much into method acting and never forgets to smear soot all over his body before rehearsals (much to the chagrin of the car hire company whose ivory-colored leather seats are now elephant grey) and considers my continual re-writes that Adam drops off for me as being entirely in synch with his own personal quest for perfection. I am very much looking forward to his performance. His understudy, on the other hand, has given up trying to memorize the continual outpouring of new lines and is resigned to concentrating on his swing roles of *Second Scab, Younger Tabloid Photographer* and *Older Tabloid Photographer*.

Anyhow, Adam's destination was a pharmaceutical conference at the Miami Hilton reporting on new treatments for the class of neurological degeneration from which I suffer—I didn't ask Adam to go, he volunteered. There's a new stem cell technique for re-coding the neurons to grow healthy tissue and bypass unhealthy mutations, which remain in your brain but are safely contained like nuclear (no pun intended) waste. Adam called it brilliant and pioneering. Of course, designing a practical application, testing it in the lab, then on animals, then on humans, getting it licensed, and also out on N.I.C.E.'s list of value-for-money NHS buys will take time. Indeed, Adam warned me that he would be surprised if more than a handful of us were still around by the end of that process.

"Well, that's what being terminally ill means." I replied sardonically. "One hasn't got long to go."

"Oh, no" corrected Adam, "I didn't mean *you*. You patients will all be long dead. I meant *us doctors*. Most delegates were over fifty; it will be our children who finalize this work. You can't rush good medical practice."

"I'm so pleased you don't work in A and E," I replied.

Anyway, the hospital that I ended up in was not for me, but for Mary. She was attending her final antenatal class and Toby couldn't make it (he was at the solicitor's completing the purchase of a Victorian terrace in Wimbledon for the family-to-be), so she sent around a taxi to get me. It was a swank private hospital in the West End. I can't tell you its name (Not for legal reasons, I can't remember it. Well my brain is dying…), but it is always in the news because film stars and sheiks' wives seem to enjoy giving birth there. And, I mean enjoy. Planned Caesareans seem in vogue for the pain-avoiding classes. Although the most pain-free birth plan of the rich and thin is still surrogacy. Avoid pregnancy as well as labor, ensure the vagina stays tight and boobs firm, and get high on prescription drugs while listening to the screams of some other financially-needy/emotionally-wrecked volunteer squeeze out the baby. I swear if Amazon.co.uk delivered babies, they would do it that way.

As it happens, Mary is planning to give birth naturally, but why she needs this five-star hotel-like environment, I know not. The equipment is the same as the NHS, the techniques are the same as the NHS, the staff is all trained by the NHS, and most of them still work (some of the week) for the NHS. So why pay all this money?

I soon realized why. It was the same reason the rich wait in executive lounges at airports, travel first class on trains, always crawl across London by car when the Tube is so much quicker, and insist on The Priory when The Maudsley is better and free. It's got nothing to do with the facilities, the service, or the staff. It's the other people. They don't want *ever* to have to rub shoulders with ordinary people. Upon this realization, I jumped into the taxi without hesitation and almost cantered to the anteroom, easily outpacing Mary. (Okay she is eight months pregnant and has all the athleticism of a heavily constipated Mr. Burns.)

The mum-to-be's class takes place in a square oak-floored chamber that is half gym and half airport multi-faith chapel. Apart from tapestries on the wall that are Chinese rural, Qiang dynasty, or reproductions of the storyboard for *Shao-Lin Nun Massacre 3D,* the only objects appear to be a set of gigantic blue inflatable balls. Like beach balls—if you were a 12-foot tall surfer—but which I assume get stuffed under the father-to-be's Katherine Hamnett T-shirt, so he can experience what it must be like to be pregnant…with eight…gorillas.

But then the midwife/facilitator/guru sits on one. My immediate shock at what appears to be a re-enactment of a new French torture movie is displaced when I realize the balls are not faux wombs, but for gently rocking on, to tighten the pelvic and abdominal muscles that assist labor. After that, I pretty much zoned out, apart from the occasion when I was addressed as young Mary's husband. I was about to retort with disparaging jokes about Michael Douglas and his Mumbles child bride (while simultaneously reassuring everyone I was a *grandfather*-to-be), but then I saw that the only other men there were even older than Michael Douglas and their female partners even younger than Catherine Zeta-Jones.

Afterwards, Mary asked what I thought and I had to reply: firstly, I thought a whole series of classes concentrating on the micro-details of labor seemed a little over the top—anyone who has seen *ER, Chicago Hope, St. Elsewhere,* or *Grey's Anatomy* knows all about women giving birth. Throw in *Junior* and you know about men giving birth, too. Secondly, labor (counted from when the contractions begin to be painful) is at most one day in the life of a mother and you spend it surrounded by dozens of professional experts. The next eighteen years raising the bugger that squeezes out, you spend on your own. Thirdly, there is absolutely nothing for a man to do at these classes or in the labor room. All that holding of hands, whispering of, "Breathe, darling," and flannelling of foreheads is both completely irrelevant and completely unnoticed. (I did thank Mary for the thoughtfulness of sending me a taxi, which I can't afford to use unless I charge it to the paper, except that ever since the ongoing financial crisis you'd be more likely to get an autograph from an amputee than a signature on your claim form.) Then the most extraordinary thing happened. Mary started shouting at me. Cuss words, too. When I say this sort of blunt stuff to Pavla she never shouts at me. Pavla either mumbles in Polish or shrugs and makes me tea. Either Mary's hormones have made her stroppy or Pavla's forbearance is not typical of other women, which brings me on to my second day out. This time, to the Polish Embassy.

Security ghosted me past a courtyard statue of Casimir the Great (That epithet being relative. I don't hear Casimir's deeds echoing through history as loudly as Alexander's, Herod's, or Peter's), where a guard in polished cuirass stood next to Pavla in the doorway of a musty office. This was painted in that institutional hue of green chosen by psychologists as the shade most likely to alleviate distress and calm tempers. Although this was a fast track, civil wedding, I did notice the presence of a cassocked priest as well as a thin-lipped registrar who looked like she was still bitter from being beaten to the part of Rosa Klebb in *From Russia with Love* by Lotte Lenya.

Also in the room was that grinning *bourgeois roué*, but now tidy and clean-shaven, fiancé of hers (for whom I will now have to come up with a new nickname). After pecking me on the cheek, Pavla locked her arm into mine. I borrowed one of Adam's suits for the occasion, not realizing that my seventies brown corduroy number counts as pretty damn chic in this particular time capsule of a building. Through some clunky box speakers, the recording of swelling vibrato vocals (which pass for soul singing today, Martha, Dionne, and Aretha must be weeping) cued our march and I escorted my friend and neighbor down the "aisle" followed by Pavla's charming maid of honor, Carolina, the manager of Starbucks at Dulwich Sainsbury's. At the back of the procession tottered "Smooth-Face's" smug girls.

We had a very pleasant meal in a Soho club afterwards— guests of Smooth Face's best man, Ralph, who has a voice as RP as Captain Jean-Luc Picard, but who was wearing a kilt, on account of his family owning half of Dumfries and Galloway (doubtless his ancestor was a Lowland traitor who fought alongside the Butcher of Cumberland at Culloden). Notwithstanding, the day moved remarkably efficiently. (The only wrinkle was when a bailiff served Smooth Face with a court order for non-payment of alimony as we were walking past a sex shop on Great Windmill Street.)

FC NAYLOR

P.S. Now you know I hate clichés even more than I hate every single page of the *Evening Standard*, but I am duty bound to mention Pavla looked very beautiful indeed in her strapless, chiffon, ruched, A-line, bridal gown with encrusted beading across the neckline and wrap-over. But then she would look be-guiling in dungarees and a duffle coat. So, congratulations, Pavla, and enjoy your month-long honeymoon, borrowing Joanna Lumley's idyllic cottage…in Bhutan. See you when you get back in time for Christmas.

39. Saturday, November 26

Got tremendous feedback for last week's column! Not from any readers, of course…from staff. And, not for the content…the word count. Cressy, Alistair, and the Directors have been in conclave all week with some private equity company in glamorous Klosters (mainly because Prince Charles' favorite Swiss resort is the only place with decent champagne within helicopter distance of the finance company's official HQ in boring Vaduz, Liechtenstein) whoring for a quick infusion of capital. Meanwhile, the top tier of newspaper staff left behind is working on a management buy-out proposal…in glamorous Kettering (mainly because the British Vauxhall Dealerships Association cancelled at the conference center attached to the race course, but I am sure the champagne is good in the winners' enclosure).

Everyone here is taking the piss. Marilyn Freud, Arts Correspondent, headlined with a rave review…of her daughter's school play. Charlie Farrell, Senior Football Correspondent, this week led with a puff piece promoting his Pub Side's upcoming fundraiser. Unbeknownst to me, and due mainly to Mr. D'Arby's continued culinary absence rather than anything else, I managed to exceed my word count by 157 percent. That's almost 1,800 words when my limit is 700. I am told on good authority this is a record unequalled since the legendary music critic (and lifetime magic mushrooms casualty) Mick Hazlitt's 1993 obituary of (his personal favorite) Frank Zappa. That ran to 12,000 words, complete with a climactic eulogy in Beat-style free verse, but was surreptitiously spread (aka hidden) across nine different pages of the newspaper, including the Property Section, which led to some very bemusing estate agent enquiries.

The other good news is that, on the basis of Adam's private renditions of my dialogue, I am very nearly settled on the final draft of *Lamplight,* which is being delivered to Mr. Eccleston and the rest of the cast as I tap. Remy, the director, has been so busy trying to source three metric tons of *papier mache* with which to sculpt the full scale escarpment that will frame the set, plus using his spare time trying to procure (for entirely professional reasons) the entire male dance ensemble from *Billy Elliot,* that he is too distracted to argue over changes in the text.

Even more cheering is the news that Adam *will* be able to see the opening of my play after all! Do not fear, North Finchley Mummers, *Guys and Dolls* has not been cancelled. The local Primary Care Trust has given Adam an ultimatum—refocus his attention immediately on his deserted surgery or be hit with a massive malpractice suit. Something had to give, so Adam decided to pull out of the musical. Esther, his wife, who ironically has now been won around to her husband's lifelong thespian ambition recommended he give up…me. This would free up his days for medical work while still keeping his evenings for his show. However, I told him to think of that poor frustrated stage manager praying for just this kind of break. So Adam, being a good sort, has now cancelled his long cherished dreams of being on stage. As I said to him, everybody wins!

I also got a postcard from Pavla, who reports that she and her new husband are having a truly unique experience in Bhutan. The only ripple being she was briefly arrested in Thimphu for joining a protest against the dominant Buddhist *Drukpa* ethnic group's discrimination against the minority Hindu *Lhotsampas.* Pavla added that it was my primary message that, "one must always say what one believes in, no matter the consequences," that inspired her to this action. Obviously, my secondary message that, "sounding your mouth off when you are the dying ex-husband of a newspaper magnate in a parliamentary democracy with a tradition of free speech that dates back to Mill, Bentham, and the

Magna Carta IS NOT THE SAME as being a vulnerable foreign visitor to a remote mountainous absolute monarchy," did not get through as clearly!

I suppose that having trumpeted such libertarian ideals, I am morally compelled to make use of this island's hard-won freedoms and put my own head on the line, publically. So here are three sincere convictions I am compelled to air. The first two are political:

1) Tony Blair, you are a lying, opportunistic, charlatan (war criminal and torturer). Like some crazed lumberjack in the rainforest, it took you ten years to destroy what had taken 150 years to develop—the entire British Labor Movement.

2) Having brought to pass Thatcher's prophecy, "There is no alternative," by manipulating the only electable opposition party (Labor) so that no alternative is ever even being expressed, you then dragged this cradle of liberty across thousands of miles on imperialist adventures in third world Iraq and Afghanistan to match those of Mussolini's in Libya and Ethiopia. Both sets of campaigns were equally lethal and incompetent, both were designed not for strategic gain, but as the coward's gambit to win the friendship of the most powerful bully in the global playground, in the former case, George W., in the latter, Adolf H. May the cries of the wounded and the blood of the dead forever deafen your unheeding ears and stain your heartless smile.

Those opinions of mine are quite public (and shared by many others). The final one is more personal and, to date, I have not revealed it to anyone:

3) Cressida, after you left me, I never put on another play, or loved another woman.

(Editor's Note: FC NAYLOR was unable to complete this column due to being taken ill after filing only part of this week's copy. He is currently undergoing treatment in Charing Cross Hospital and we wish him well. Meanwhile, Ferdinand D'Arby returns with a recipe for winter that combines "the adolescent zest of shallots with the New

World honesty of fennel seeds, forthright lusty Merlot, and casually seductive oyster mushrooms with baby cauliflower and freshly slaughtered Canadian caribou to conjure a meal fit for a truly discerning pioneer of the North West Passage.)"

In the meantime, Mr. Naylor has consented to the publication of a collection of his diary entries in book form, which should be on the shelves before Christmas!

40. Thursday, November 30

What prescience, what prolepsis of such Aristophanic coincidence; Thomas Hardy would have been proud. I gloat about visiting a hospital on behalf of someone other than myself and one week later, an ambulance, a Hippocratic chariot, carries me to one in a parlous state.

I was very impressed they found room for me without an appointment, what with half the population convulsing dementedly with VCJD from all that infected beef, and the rest either hemorrhaging from the Ebola virus, spluttering to death from SARS, or supine and feverish from flus, both Avian and Swine flavored. Indeed, I am shocked that such a rapid series of recent lethal pandemics has not finished the job that the Black Death started in the fourteenth century. But then, maybe those regular announcements of imminent viral Armageddon—repeated in this very paper, among others—were a tad inflated in retrospect. I mean, when millenarians Blessing and Eunice from *The Watchtower* are describing them as scare mongering, it might be time to sound a note of cautious scepticism.

I had a scare, though. My cerebellum overheated (did you know that *bellum* is Latin for *war* and *cere* is the root word for *grain*? Cornflake wars are going on in our heads). Anyway, I have been awarded this special weekday column rather than waiting 'til Saturday, so I can let readers know, many of whom have shown an interest, primarily on the newspaper comment blog (I was wondering why the letters were drying up. I didn't realize there was a blog.), in the results of my daughter-in-common-law's confinement. Yes, Mary went into labor while at an all-day pop concert and was so insistent on hearing the head-liner—some R & B act who seems unwilling to sing one note when she can sing ten instead—that by the time of the last encore, Mary was too far gone to get to her private clinic and was whisked into the local A and E with Naylor Jr. already crowning.

In fact, Mary almost had it in the taxi. Luckily, the driver was willing to put his foot down even if he did jump two sets of lights and rear-ended some knob's Mercedes CLS Coupe, whose passenger ended up in the same local NHS hospital for quite different reasons! Ha, ha! So much for the rich avoiding the Hoi Poloi by virtue of their luxury, private health schemes and private elective Caesareans! How do I know all this? Because the bandaged bloke's trolley almost collided with ours in the corridor!

Toby was there with Mary and a few moments later, we were joined by Frances Naylor. Two generations became three. Mary was in tears—less for sentiment and more due to the pain of a rapidly stitched up episiotomy. Toby was in tears too and then Cressida turned to pour her tributary of tears into the lake of lachrymosity. I, on the other hand, was laughing my head off. Not due to the irony of Mary's discomfort—do not confuse the sardonic with the cruel—nor with relief at squeezing out enough extra days to witness the birth of a grandchild. My mirth is due to the same thing that is behind the (even more than usual) lax logic of this rambling column. Morphine.

What a rush! I have never been much of a recreational drug user, Single Malt and Champagne Truffle topping the menu of adult treats. My position on mood enhancers has always been that downers were for fifties housewives, dope and acid for sixties hippies, smack for seventies punks, coke for eighties yuppies, ecstasy for the dancing zombies of the nineties, and today's drugs (Crystal meth, Oxycontin, Crack, Ket, GBL, etc., etc.) the bankrupt currency of school playgrounds and sink estates.

So, I never fitted in, but this morphine stuff made me reconsider all those much maligned nineteenth century Unequal

Treaties we imposed on China after the Opium Wars, and I have *never been more* opposed to the West's occupation of Afghanistan than now, if it means endangering just one poppy field. I can now see why in this secular century, religion has been replaced by opium as the, er, opium of the people…

There is not much to say about baby Frances. You can tell from the name *Frances* that she is a girl, thereby proving the "best Ultrasound scan that insurance premiums can buy" to be as accurate as all those apocalyptic public health warnings I alluded to earlier. The baby's name, albeit not identical to mine (clue as to what the *F* in FC stands for), is allegedly Toby's testament to me. Although sadly, my patronym will never be able to converse with the man himself since my doctors do not expect me to last much longer. Shame, as you know how I love a captive audience. So, I have decided to leave little Frances all my manuscripts, should she wish to mug up on what it was her grandfather had to say that he insisted was so important for others to hear…

I must now announce that very soon, dear reader, our own conversation must cease, too. For in amongst the jubilation at the arrival of another member of the human race (a celebration that can only be vindicated in retrospect, given that the state of simply "being born" is neither a virtue nor a vice, and on today's exhausted and overpopulated planet requires a lifetime of good deeds to offset the additional consumption of finite resources that extra life entails), Cressida confessed that the financial summit in Switzerland had failed. The paper is to fold (no pun intended) after next week.

Hopefully, my final column will coincide with the opening of *Lamplight* and a few of my words will continue to travel in the air a few days or weeks after their extinction on the page, even if most of them will be spoken by a Time Lord from Gallifrey. Advance ticket sales are doing very well, although most of the customers seem to be trading-card enthusiasts aged between eight and fourteen or unwaged adult bachelors (likewise eligible for concessions), who have Internet usernames such as *Servelans_Gimp*, *7of9s-Slave*, and *RoseTylerzzz-Hot*—the last of which is not to be confused with a similarly named minor character from Shakespeare (and major character from Stoppard).

FC Naylor (Grandfather)

P.S. You may notice that I have not informed you, as is custom, of baby Frances' birth weight because I cannot see its purpose. Indeed, in this age of obesity and eating disorders to be introduced by name, sex, and *body mass* seems particularly inauspicious. And, the subsequent habit of tacking on the precise number of weeks or months they have been on the planet doesn't help either. I, for one, wouldn't like to be presented to friends as "FC Naylor, male, eleven and a half stone, 700 months on Sunday!" I know you wouldn't like it and I am sure babies don't like it either. It might even be the reason they always cry... "Let me see, why is she still crying? Nappy dry, just had a refreshing sleep, ate well, burped successfully, no temperature." The infant's thoughts reply, "Because you won't stop going on about my bloody *weight and age* all the time!"

41. December 3 - FC NAYLOR'S FINAL COLUMN (dictated from his hospital bed)

Stop the press!

I have always wanted to say that and I am saying it—literally saying it—as I am dictating this final column. My arm is not working as I would like, but my voice remains as loud and clear as ever. And, hey, I am a man of ideas not a squash player, so bugger the arm. No golfing holidays in Spain for me; at the club every other Sunday while the wife cooks the roast and I look forward to three hours of Formula One on TV—the life of many of my peers, but not of FC. Not then, not now, not ever.

You may have gathered by now that this is an officially extended column, twice the usual size like a series finale in an American TV drama series. TV—why do I keep mentioning it; the theatre was my medium, not the box? Was…and possibly is again, for last night was the opening night of *Lamplight,* and today (your today, not my today as I am writing this yesterday, so I will not be able to pass on what the reviews were like since this newspaper has no tomorrow), the reviews will decide the fate of my play. My legacy. Cancel or run? Close tonight or continue?

"But wait," I hear you say—well, those of you who have read previous editions and are also very camp and theatrical *might* say that. Are you reading, Simon Callow? "Wait, just one bit and don't stereotype me, Naylor," I hear you add. "You said advance sales were going very well because of Christopher Eccleston being so popular, so how can you talk of the play closing after one night?"

Well, yes, I did say that, and Mr. Eccleston remains popular and deservedly so. Unfortunately, he isn't in the play. Not anymore.

You know the expression, "Break a leg," that is quoted to confer good luck on actors, well I don't know if someone accidentally said, "Macbeth!" backstage or what, but breaking a leg is exactly what Eccleston did. Or rather, I did…to him. That posh silver Mercedes we rammed getting Mary to hospital with the well-dressed passenger inside…that was him…and I am terribly sorry, and Frances is too. Well, she will be when she is old enough to be told the story of her birth and the fractured femur it caused to my leading man.

Anyway, that was on Wednesday. Dress rehearsal on Thursday has no Underwood—the main part—so I show up to help sort out the crisis and the director is not pleased. Nevertheless, being a professional and my benefactor, gang master Kristof being out on remand now and demanding the show go ahead—I understand he needs some revenue pronto to pay his legal fees—the understudy, Oscar, is summoned to go on. Trouble is, the bugger doesn't know his lines. Well, not *these* lines anyway. Oscar is familiar with the *original* lines, but none of my extensive rewrites of all of Underwood's speeches. Of course, Remy's idea is to have Oscar use the old script for opening night and then rehearse him next week.

Well, I may not be here next week, and the play may have closed by next week—I want my words, the up-to-date proper words spoken right now. It almost led to blows between Remy and myself. He was pontificating that a good director should be master of the script not its slave. "Theatre is more than just words alone." I replied that if people exited from Youtube, quit wasting hours tagging their Facebook photos, put down f***ing *Call of Duty 4,* and picked up a sodding book once in a while, our gasping craven, shallow, culture that makes Sodom and Gomorrah look like Athens and Alexandria might stand a chance of revival. Then Remy called me a medieval cultural Luddite and I told him that Luddism did not emerge until 1813 in

Nottingham, whereas the consensus is that the medieval period had ended by 1485, after which came the Renaissance. Then Remy called me a prehistoric, washed-up hack too insecure to allow another artist to reinterpret his lines and I called him an effete old c**t who should direct the Teletubbies if he can't handle speech. Then Kristof got out some matches to burn the theater down for the insurance when a voice piped up.

"I know the lines…the new up-to-date lines."

It's Adam. He gave me a lift to the theatre because Pavla is still in the Himalayas. And that's how it was resolved. Adam stepped in. He had said the new lines out loud to me often enough. Plus, for most of the play, you don't actually see Underwood anyway. He's trapped himself at the bottom of the mine, disabled the winch, and is on a hunger strike until the Coal Board re-opens it. You hear his voice, but it comes out of the darkness, the darkness that he and the men of the village have spent their lives working in, so the rest of us can have light. The only light you can see on stage is the flame of the lamp he wears on his helmet and nothing else. Hence, the title, *Lamplight*. And this light fades more and more as the play goes on, until by the end, the light, and with it, all hope for his people and for his own life, dies out too.

Well, you may ask, if Underwood is never seen why couldn't Oscar the understudy simply read the revised script from the wings? Why do you need the amateur Adam? Because, at the very end of the play Underwood emerges, slowly climbing out of the Stygian gloom. He is a ghost now, a spectral martyr, but still a giant figure, a symbol of resistance, of unending struggle against the lies, the hypocrisy, the vanity, and the greed. Against that easy bloody surrender, served like milk to babes, to occasion bloated slumber. And my oldest friend, Dr. Adam Gold, really is a giant-winged angel of a man who has never given up on me even when I gave up on myself, and if his dream is to walk onto a stage…then so he shall.

And, he did. Cressida came to see it and Toby, too. (I wouldn't let Mary in with the baby, noisy little devil child; don't want her spoiling my big night.) Oh, and I wouldn't let Alistair in either. He's not that bad a bloke, really, but he is my boss and is screwing my ex-wife, so that Scotch bastard can stay at home, too.

On the way out, after the curtain call and the flowers for Remy (no cries of "author, author," though), and my patron producer Kristof is missing…along with all the takings from the box office and concession stands, I encountered one more surprise—Pavla.

"You guys came home early from your honeymoon just to see my play!" I exclaimed, moved.

"No. We got deported because *you* encouraged my wife to take part in a demonstration," spat the suntanned, bourgeois spouse. "Oh, and we only landed at Gatwick two hours ago, so actually we missed your great oeuvre," he added smugly.

Pavla, however, reassured me that the curtailing of their holiday was not my fault. However, it was true that she had missed the play that she had been so instrumental in setting up for me. And given that we had to refund at short notice all the Dr. Who fans who had block-booked the first week, bleeding us dry of all our advance sales, the *only* chance of a second night, which Pavla can attend, is if this morning's reviews are good enough to bring in some new punters. (Adam has volunteered to continue the run, passing only on the weekday matinee so he does not have to miss any of his surgeries.)

"But don't worry if you miss it, Pavla," I reassured her. "As a Pole, you must have mixed feelings about the British Miners' Strike. Remember how I told you that as a direct consequence of Thatcher closing *our* pits, that we now import most of our coal from *your* country."

She shook her head. "My country is your country now," she said flashing her ring.

"The entire world is all one country, as far as I am concerned."

I went on to explain why I could never countenance protectionism. The social imperative is not about preserving British jobs, per se, but preserving all jobs. If some of our internal jobs transfer to poorer countries abroad as a result of globalization, I am all in favor of it. The urban working class and rural poor of developing countries need jobs as much as we do. It's not *where* the job is that counts, it is the pay and conditions of that job that matter, so that no worker of any nationality is exploited. I explained that the defeat of the NUM wasn't just about local working traditions being mothballed. A lot of miners hate bloody mining—it's grim, painful, and unsafe.

It is about being lied to, robbed, bullied, and left with nothing. It is about being allowed no power over your own destiny. It is about the end of solidarity and collective struggle in our country. The Labour Party was annihilated in 1983, the Women's Movement splintered, and the Trades Unions were emasculated. The Youth Movement was silenced. Instead of joining together to make things better for those around, by the late eighties everybody went completely into themselves. The ruling class stayed on the same course accumulating personal wealth and the liberal Bourgeoisie retired from public life and took up New Age vegan diets, homeopathy, yoga, chanting, reflexology, and counselling. It became all about yourself, *your* body, *your* spirit, and *your* mind. The material conditions of others were completely ignored.

That's why when the Tories got tired in 1997, New Labor was ready to come off the subs' bench and continue the match with hardly anyone even noticing the difference. Now everybody is plugged into an iPod or Bluetooth, or staring at a game console or laptop updating their *personal* page dedicated entirely to themselves. They never have to see anyone else. The working class are being seduced by racists and xenophobes to turn against fellow workers of a different religion or nation, and distracted by the price of moat-dredging, toilet seats and duck houses while the real crime, the exploitation of surplus value of their labor, is going all around them.

I say look up from your electronic toys and Broadband opiates. Wake up from the false consciousness of Reality TV and gossip magazines. Seek out your allies and unite. And to those allies, I say this, do not allow yourselves to be turned against each other, deliberately crashed into one another, by the self serving Flavio Briatore's of the ruling class and its agents in the media.

To my comrades, the **Greens,** I say, searching for the best *alternative* energy source to replace fossil fuels is like searching for a *more humane* form of capital punishment. In the eighteenth century it gave us the Guillotine, in the twentieth, the lethal injection, when all executions are wrong. So stop chasing rainbows. We must reduce per capita consumption as well as aggregate population or the only answer is scarcity. Or, colonizing the moon.

To my comrades, the **Blacks,** I say, in the last three years, more young black males have been killed by other young black males in English cities than were killed by the KKK in the whole of the Deep South throughout the '50s and '60s. In the names of Malcolm and Martin, you are not avatars in *Manhunt* or extras in a music video, and there are no "Fallen Souljahs," only prisons and graves filled with black kids. Do your homework; get active in politics and you shall achieve the respect you are owed.

To my comrades, the **Women,** I say, the glass ceiling you are trying to break overlooks the wrong room. Your ambition to outrace the men to the Boardrooms of the FTSE 100 is as misplaced as going for Playground Pusher of the Year. Profiting through exploiting your female workforce and conning your female customers while underpaying migrant women to look after your kids is more Imelda Marcos or Margaret Thatcher than Mary Wollstonecraft or Simone de Beauvoir. Replacing the warders does not free the prisoners. Raise the aspirations of girls in school and the status and pay of women who care, clean, and cater for a living. F**k sexism in the city and in chambers. Tear them down.

To my comrades, the **Workers,** I say, don't turn on your brothers and sisters from poorer countries to protect "your" jobs. How can you begrudge those who have even less than you, the means to pay for their families? Join with them and make sure ALL workers are paid the same for the same job—the highest rate—raising their standards to yours will stop the profiteers undercutting you.

To my comrades, the **Liberal Bourgeoisie,** I say, if you pay for private health care or private schools, hold shares, or rent out second homes, you are the problem not the solution. Use your education and professional skills for the public good instead of voting like the students of 1968 while living like the landlords of 1868.

To my comrades, the **Soldiers,** I say, there is less chance of imposing a unitary, democratic State based on sexual equality and non-violent rule of law in Afghanistan than of Mel Gibson circumcising himself at a Bris. Lay down your weapons, scoop up a kilo of opium, and use the proceeds to start a loft insulation business back home. Everyone will be better off.

To my comrades, the **Muslims,** I say, the Umma is the biggest community in the Third World. You have the power to change your world from one of poverty and corruption into one of liberty and equality, yet you drape women in linen cages and cast heretics at Improvised Explosive Devices in an Afro-Asian reboot of the European Counter Reformation. (I agree, *The Satanic Verses* was a really annoying book, though.) Do not simply parrot that Allah is merciful. Exercise that mercy.

To my comrades, the **Chinese,** I say, you overthrew feudal warlords and resisted Japanese invaders. Too wise to embrace the Europe of the sixteenth century (see above), you have instead adopted the Europe of the nineteenth, instead with your wide screen version of the Industrial Revolution school of capitalism. I guess all that censorship of Western culture must have been successful then, for not a word of Dickens or Zola seems to have made it to the Far East. You are the biggest nation in the world; nourish it, do not eat it up.

To my comrades, the **Americans,** I say, if you spent on public taxes what you instead choose to spend on handguns in your homes, you could pay for universal healthcare and still have enough left over to clothe the whole country in cowboy hats, if that is the look you like. If you channelled the money you spend on pornography, drugs, gambling, and junk food, you could clothe the entire world in cowboy hats. You are the richest country in the world; don't throw it all away on sweets.

My tiny voice says all these things, but who is listening? And, if it is too weak and quiet to reach all my comrades, then I shall be grateful if it only reaches you. Then perhaps you can use *your* voices to spread my words once I have gone. Or, maybe, if those blasted reviews are good enough (I think one of those Australasian freebie magazines had someone in), my words will still be heard after the column finishes today, in *Lamplight*. Through Adam on the stage, Pavla if she gets to see the show, my son Toby, or Baby Frances…

But, I fear, no longer through me.

For my body is to cease publication today. The VHD has withered it and I have been told that Death awaits me. And, yet, I must demur—not on medical grounds or because of any recently acquired clairvoyant power (like painter Isaac in *Heroes,* I'm sure they make that show up as they go along), but because that statement has no meaning. To ascribe death with transitive power, to reify, to give presence and intent to what by definition is absence, makes no sense. As for the scythe, cloak, and Swedish accent, well, that persuades even less than personifying evil in the form of a clown. (Clowns are not scary; they're just *not funny.*) So what does lie ahead?

Nothing. Oblivion without resurrection and without judgement—whatever number of seals and trumpets, riders and angels, heads, whores, and horns. No suffering or enlightenment, no infernal circles, no Valhalla of feasting and fighting, no Nirvana of non-corporeal, extra-dimensional blissful grace, no reincarnation as a cockroach or a Canadian, no return visits for teatime séances, no Halloween guest appearances on *Most Haunted,* nor ghostly groping of a semi-naked Demi Moore. No solace or easeful anything. Dreamless, purposeless sleep, final exit to nowhere from a random, Godless universe.

Fortunately, the Voltaire's Hippocampic Disorder that steered me toward this terminus afflicts the brain rather than the heart. I know that people say that when you are young your heart rules your life, and when you get older it is your head. I know that people say by the age of thirty-five, everyone forsakes their ideals for a mortgage, a pension, and school fees. And I don't disagree; however, I think this conservative, selfish caution is simply one more phase in one's life, but not the final one. It does not have to last forever. Why do you think so many millionaires in their later years leave their money to their pets? As you approach death as I do, the wheel may turn once more, their hearts rise again, and all that "maturity" and "wisdom" dismissed as a false epiphany. In some cases, this spring-like re-awakening expresses itself in buying a stupidly large motor bike, putting a gold sleeper back in your ear, and reforming Mott the Hoople, but it does not have to be that way.

For me, this phase has led me not only to articulate new words, but also to hear old ones once more. Words first spoken long ago, at last heard clearly again, no longer muted by the mental fog of age. Words that can lift a person above the confining wall of circumstance and scale the ladder to his liberation. My words, your words, other people's words. Words echoing back through time, not in faded reproduction, but restored, as clear and commanding as the muezzin at sunrise, urging us never to forget that, "It is better to die on your feet than live on your knees," even after two hip replacements; that, "You can take away my life, but you cannot take away my freedom"; "Workers of the world unite, you have nothing to lose but your satellite dishes"; "...and he who will fall is he who has stalled"; "Now those bloody bells have started. Stop ringing those bells!"; "Hey, Johnny, what are you rebelling against?"; "What have you got?"; "Meet the new boss. Same as the old boss!"; "I coulda been a contender, a somebody"; "I am Spartacus"; "It's getting dark, tooooo dark to see—feels like I'm knocking on heaven's door"; "Eloi, Eloi, lama sabachthani!"; She canna take it, Captain!"; "Morituri te salutant"; "Now cracks a noble heart"; and "Here's looking at you, kid!"

The rest is silence.

FC Naylor

Epilogue

Playwright and columnist, FC Naylor lapsed into a coma in the early hours of the morning of December 3, a state in which he remains to this day.

FC never found out that there were no reviews of *Lamplight,* since there had not been any press in the audience. The Antipodeian girl whom he thought was from *TNT* magazine was actually a barmaid from Walkabout across the road. The cast did perform the play, unpaid, one more time…for Pavla's sake. (And also because Kristof, in a telegram from Northern Cyprus, threatened that if they did not, no Pole would ever do their plumbing, painting, or carpentry ever again.)

Recently, the secret of his name was revealed. FC stands for Francis Churchill. It was "Naylor" that was the pseudonymous affectation. It was chosen in tribute to the outspoken radical Quaker, James Nayler who, in 1656, had his tongue pierced with a hot iron by order of Britain's military government, as punishment for blasphemy.

FC Naylor's true surname sleeps with him.

Follow the further adventures of FC Naylor on
www.deadmantalking1.blogspot.com